THE LOVE OF GODS

THE LOVE OF GODS

Alan Hunter

Chivers Press • Thorndike Press
Bath, England   Thorndike, Maine USA

15174640

This Large Print edition is published by Chivers Press, England and by Thorndike Press, USA.

Published in 1998 in the U.K. by arrangement with Constable & Company Ltd.

Published in 1998 in the U.S. by arrangement with Constable & Company Ltd.

U.K. Hardcover ISBN 0–7540–3162–4 (Chivers Large Print)
U.S. Softcover   ISBN 0–7862–1288–8 (General Series Edition)

The text of this Large Print edition is unabridged.
Other aspects of the book may vary from the original edition.

Set in 16 pt. New Times Roman.

Printed in Great Britain on acid-free paper.

British Library Cataloguing in Publication Data available

Library of Congress Catalog Card Number: 97-91166

ISBN: 0–7862–1288–8 (lg. print: sc)

CHAPTER ONE

'Would have bored me stiff,' Sir Tommy said. 'That Beresford fellow is the wife's cousin. Met him somewhere. I'm told he's made a pile, but I'm damned if I've read any of his books.'

'Spy-thrillers.' Reymerston grinned.

'Well, there you are,' Sir Tommy said. 'MI5, not my pigeon. Not that I'd read the damned things if they were. Who else was there?'

'Oh, the usual crowd. Would-be writers, painters, actors.'

Sir Tommy clicked his tongue. 'Amateurs.'

'More or less,' Reymerston admitted. 'But our young poet had just had his first book published and you couldn't call my colleague Chris Clarke an amateur. It's true he makes his living from bread-and-butter stuff—fishing-boats, beachscapes, Wolmering street scenes, but if you're a young painter without private means you don't have very much option.'

'Is he any good?'

'Yes, I think so. Give him time. He's only thirty.'

'And the poet fellow?'

Reymerston made a face. 'I'm only a painter. You had better ask Alec.'

'And every month this gang gets together?'

'Every month,' Reymerston said. 'A soirée of the local talent rubbing shoulders at Alec's

1

place. It was his idea. He gave some talks and it followed on from there. I got roped in to judge the paintings and I've been turning up ever since. Sometimes, as you say, it can be a bore, but old Alec isn't mean with the hospitality.'

Sir Tommy shook his head. 'Just don't ask me there!'

'You, you're as bad as George!' Reymerston grinned.

'Was he invited?'

'Just the once. And he pleaded a previous engagement.'

Gently stirred in his deck-chair and tipped his hat a little further over his eyes.

All this was happening in the garden at Heatherings on a sunny Sunday afternoon in June. They had invited the Capels and the Reymerstons to join them for afternoon tea. The Doctor and his wife sat chatting with Gabrielle at the table, set in the shade of the beech tree, while Ruth Reymerston basked on a sun-bed, also with her hat pulled over her eyes. And the Chief Constable . . . He'd been over to Wolmering to appear at some function that required his presence, from which he had gracefully retired to seek relaxation with the Gentlys. It often happened. He lived only six miles off. His car was a familiar presence in their drive. Now he sat sipping a drink, also parked in a deck-chair, and gassing convivially with Andy Reymerston.

Overhead, twittering martins glided to their

nests under the eaves, while, through a gate in the beech hedge, one could see already a trace of colour in the bell-heather. And there were butterflies about the snapdragon, hovering dragonflies, bees ... Were there ever moments more peaceful than those spent here, in their garden at Heatherings?

'But what do you actually do at these meetings, that's what I would like to know.'

'Oh—this and that.' Reymerston sighed and reached for his glass. 'People show their paintings, read things, tell each other about what they're doing. Then we may have a bit of acting. Last night, for example, there was a play-reading.'

'A play-reading?'

'People write them you know. And then we try them out at Alec's. We had Derek Hopkins there, from the town's Little Theatre, he chose a cast and managed it all.' Reymerston drank broodingly. 'But it was our poet who was the hero of the evening. He had copies of his book, which he was signing for people, and afterwards gave readings from it. Then he was cast as the lead in the play, though that didn't go down well with everyone. He had a love scene with Chris's girl-friend, Liz, and Chris didn't think a lot of that.'

'Any ructions?'

Reymerston shook his head. 'We're civilised people, old lad. Chris gave her a few dirty looks, then he cleared off and left them to it.

3

Ambrose, that's our poet, is quite a looker, but I don't think Liz was losing her head.'

'My God, it sounds dull,' Sir Tommy said. 'Did no one get boozed, or throw a tantrum?'

'Not a soul.'

'And you call that being civilised?'

'For want of a better word.' Reymerston grinned.

Ruth Reymerston trailed a hand on the grass. 'I like Ambrose,' she said dreamily. 'He *looks* the part, a young Shelley or something. And he's always polite in the shop.'

'He works in some damned shop?' Sir Tommy said.

'In the bookshop in town.'

'His father is West, the estate agent,' Reymerston said. 'But selling houses doesn't cut much ice with Ambrose.'

'He's handsome,' Ruth Reymerston said. 'He has gingerish hair and light-brown eyes. A bit Rupert Brookish, you might say. If I were Chris I think I'd watch out.'

'Nonsense, old girl. He's too young for Liz.'

'They are never too young,' Ruth Reymerston mused. 'But no doubt you know best. You see more of these people than I do.'

Reymerston lofted a shoulder and drank.

'I, I too like this poet,' Gabrielle said, moving across from her seat at the table. 'George, we have met him, the young man in the bookshop who took so much trouble to get the book I wanted. You are remembering?'

Gently grunted.

'Yes, he is nice,' Gabrielle said. 'I think. I must buy his book and he shall sign it for me. I will go into town tomorrow.'

'Don't expect too much.' Reymerston grinned. 'I've heard him read some of it, remember.'

'Blasted tripe, no doubt,' Sir Tommy said. 'These days they've forgotten how it's done.'

'Aha, but I shall buy it,' Gabrielle said. 'Who knows. Tomorrow this young man may be famous.'

'Don't bank on it, Gabby.'

'But the book I shall have. And now, who is wanting another drink?'

Glasses were refilled. Gently lit his pipe. The conversation shifted to other topics. And still the martins flittered overhead and butterflies hovered above the blossoms . . .

He wasn't expected back in town till the Tuesday and, as far as he knew, no urgent business was awaiting him. He had come down here to relax and that was what he meant to do, letting even the conversation drift by him. Last week had been a tough one. He'd been up at all hours, locked in interminable interrogations, in fact had only put the case to bed as dawn was rising on that Saturday morning. They'd travelled up by train, he couldn't face a drive, and Mrs Jarvis had fetched them from the station. And now, even after an early night, all he wanted was to loaf and let the world drift by.

5

Was he getting old? No . . . just tired! There were limits and he had run up against one . . .

He rose and went down to the gate, leant there staring at the Walks beyond, taking it in, letting his mind empty, allowing the pipe to grow cold in his mouth. Behind him he could hear the talk and laughter, the strident comments of Sir Tommy. Before him, the heather slopes fell away, with rashes of purple among the brown. Already the heather was scenting. Small blue butterflies explored it. In another month, the whole wide vale would carry colour to the horizon. He leaned and gazed, breathed in the perfume, let time pass him as it would.

Vaguely, he became aware of something different, a change in the voices behind him. A fresh voice. A voice he knew: he didn't need to look round. He felt a moment of anger. The voice was that of the officer i/c of the local CID, Chief Inspector Eyke, a likeable enough fellow, but out of place here. Why had he come? He was talking to Sir Tommy, with the others occasionally joining in. Resolutely, Gently kept his back to the lawn, his eyes fixed on the slopes of heather. It wasn't him they wanted. No! If Eyke had come here, it was after Sir Tommy . . . But then he heard steps approaching, steps that he identified, again without looking round.

'Old man, I'm afraid there's a flap on . . .'

It was Capel they had sent to fetch him.

'What—sort of a flap?'

'You're not going to believe this, but it's about that poet fellow. He went missing last night and they've only just caught up with him, in the shrubbery in Alec Beresford's garden.'

Gently stared at the distance. 'So?'

'Sir Tommy wants you along, old man.'

'The fellow was dead?'

'I'm afraid so. He had been battered with a fencing-stake.'

* * *

No one was sitting down now. They stood about Sir Tommy in a shocked group. Eyke, looking somewhat embarrassed, stood a little aside from the others. Clearly he had been caught on the hop: he was dressed in a T-shirt and jeans. Probably he, too, had been lounging in his garden when the call came through to drag him away. Ruth Reymerston was in tears; Capel's wife, Tanya, was holding her arm. Andy himself was staring incredulously; Gabrielle with tightly pressed lips. And Sir Tommy with a face of thunder . . .

'Goddamn it, George! Would you credit it?'

Gabrielle moved to Gently's side, placed her hand on his arm.

'Do we know when it happened?' Gently asked.

'Last night, sir,' Eyke said. 'Some time before midnight, the doctor says. His parents

7

got in touch when they found he hadn't come home, but it had happened before, so they weren't too worried.'

'Who found him?'

'Mr Beresford. After lunch he took his coffee out to a bench near the shrubbery. Then something caught his eye, the young fellow's briefcase, and he went to pick it up. And then he saw him.'

'And—the stake?'

'That was lying there beside him. Mr Beresford said he didn't touch anything, just went straight in and rang us.'

'You have been to the scene?'

'Yes, sir. The gravel was a bit scruffed. The stake is rough wood, I doubt if we'll get very much from that. The men are out there now conducting a search, but Mr Beresford insisted I get in touch with Sir Thomas.'

'Blast him!' Sir Tommy interrupted. 'Blast him. Does he think I'm going to take over the inquiry?'

'Said you were a relative, sir.'

'The cheeky so-and-so!'

'Said he was a cousin of your wife's.'

'Ha!' Sir Tommy jerked his head. 'Well, I suppose I shall have to see the fellow. But that's all. It's up to you, Eykey. No wife's cousin is going to drag me into this.'

Eyke hesitated. 'He did mention, sir—' His eye found Gently, then switched away.

'Oh, did he then.' Sir Tommy stared at

8

Gently. 'Then perhaps the fellow isn't such a fool after all. But it's all the same. I'm not lumbering poor George. He comes here to get a break from affairs like this. You can handle it, Eykey?'

'Oh yes, sir!'

'So that's how it's going to stay. Unless—' He paused, eyeing Gently narrowly. 'Unless George cares to sit in for a couple of rounds. What do you say, George?'

Gently's face was expressionless. He could feel Gabrielle's hand pressing his arm. And Andy Reymerston's eye was on him, an eye earnest with appeal.

'Well?'

'I'm due back on Tuesday—'

'Oh, I can fix that,' Sir Tommy said. 'I'll give the Yard a ring tomorrow. I suppose Gilly will be in by then?'

Gently shrugged.

'Please!' Gabrielle said. 'That poor young man. We met him, remember.'

'Do it as a favour, George,' Reymerston urged. 'Don't forget that I'm mixed up in this too.'

Was there any option? And yet . . .

'If you want me to, I will sit in.'

'Then that's settled,' Sir Tommy said. 'I'll ring my wife, then we'll get along and talk to that fellow.'

'I had better come too,' Reymerston said. 'I saw as much of what went on last night as

9

anybody.'

There was a general move towards the house. Gently hesitated, still lingered on the lawn. Gabrielle glanced back at him: he sighed, knocked out his pipe. And followed the others.

* * *

From Heatherings to Wolmering was a matter of seven miles. Eyke led the way in his wife's Escort, pursued by Sir Tommy's Jag and Reymerston's Renault. Gently drove with Sir Tommy. There was little said between them. Sir Tommy's face had a bleak expression. They threaded the cluttered High Street of the small town and descended the road that led to the harbour. And there, on high ground to the left, almost hidden by trees, stood a handsome house, reached by a drive. Eyke signalled a turn through the gates, but then stood on his brakes, bringing an oath from Sir Tommy. Out of the drive had emerged an ambulance, to head back up towards the town.

'I suppose ...?'

Gently shook his head.

'Well, the blasted doctor can give us the details!'

Sir Tommy sent the Jag after the Escort, up a drive that wound between tall trees. At the top there was spacious parking, already occupied by a couple of patrol-cars. Several uniform-men stood about, and two plain-

10

clothes officers whom Gently recognised. Sir Tommy slammed the Jag in on the heels of the Escort. Reymerston drifted alongside. They climbed out. Eyke was already consulting with one of the men.

'Nothing?'

'Sorry, sir. We've been all over . . .'

The photographer had presumably come and gone. As a matter of course, a fence of tapes had been erected around a rustic arch away to the right. Sir Tommy stared grimly about him, at the front and steps of the Edwardian house. Then his eye fell on an oak bench, situated beneath a trailing laburnum.

'Is that it?'

'Yes, sir. Mr Beresford . . .'

Sir Tommy stalked over to the bench and sat down on it. He eyed the tapes, the rustic arch. The latter gave access through a trimmed yew hedge beyond which the beginning of a gravel path was visible.

'And he saw this briefcase, did he?'

'Yes, sir. We found it lying like he said, just inside there. It had some books in it, books of poetry. I sent it in to be checked for dabs.'

'You could see it from here.'

'Oh yes, sir. He took me here and showed me.'

Sir Tommy grunted. He looked round for Gently, then rose and advanced towards the arch. Gently followed, with Eyke in the rear. They negotiated the tapes. Beyond the arch was a circular area of flowering shrubs and some beds of begonias. The gravel path encircled the enclosure and there were two more benches, like that by the house. The yew hedge enclosed the area completely and there had been attempts at topiary behind the benches.

'And . . . that's the spot?'

There could be no question. The bloodied gravel pointed it out. And, around it, the scarred gravel offered indication of a violent act.

'How was he lying?'

'On his face, sir, like he'd been struck from behind. But from the state of him he must have been struck some more after that.'

'No doubt that chummie meant to finish him.'

Eyke shook his head. 'No doubt at all, sir.'

'Where was the stake?'

'Thrown down beside him. It was the one chummie had pulled out from the bed there.'

Sir Tommy went to stare at the hole. The stake had been one of several used in training the shrubs. They were old, weathered, roughened with lichen, and offered small hope of preserving prints.

'You've searched him?'

Eyke nodded.

'Well?'

'He hadn't been robbed, sir. His wallet was still there. It had fifty quid in it, besides a

12

couple of credit cards.'

'Just . . . somebody wanted him dead.'

'That's the way I'm seeing it, sir.'

'Some sod whom he had crossed-up.'

'Yes, sir. That's who we shall be after.'

Sir Tommy swung round. 'Any comment, George?'

But at that moment they were interrupted. A stocky, bearded man had appeared under the arch. He stood staring at them with worried eyes, his hands working nervously. Finally the eyes fixed on Sir Tommy and he took a couple of faltering steps forward.

'It's you . . . it is you?'

Sir Tommy shrugged. 'Yes, it bloody is!'

'Oh, thank heaven. Thank heaven!'

And he reached out to grab Sir Tommy's unwilling hand.

* * *

'Let's go inside shall we?'

'Yes—yes. Anything!'

Alec Beresford was about fifty and perhaps a head shorter than Gently. He had a mop of greying hair and the beard was hiding a stubborn jaw-line. He had a prominent nose and brown eyes beneath unusually bushy eyebrows, and spoke with a low, gravelly voice that seemed to come out of his chest.

'You can't understand . . .'

'Let's just go in.'

13

'I felt that if only you . . .'

'Keep it, I tell you!'

'But you must see . . .'

Sir Tommy almost propelled him up the steps.

They entered a tiled hall from windows at the end of which one saw the sea. Landscape paintings adorned its walls, one at least the work of Reymerston. Beresford led them down it. From a door on the right one heard the sound of voices. Beresford hesitated, then finally knocked before throwing open the door. It admitted them to a spacious lounge, furnished in art nouveau style, where sat a blonde lady, with a young man beside her and Reymerston in close attendance. Beresford ushered them in.

'My dear . . . Sir Thomas!'

Nervously, the blonde lady extended her hand.

'My wife, Melanie . . . and this is Lesley, our son. But I'm afraid . . .' He glanced awkwardly at Gently.

'Oh, she knows all about him!' Reymerston said. 'I have just been putting Melanie in the picture. Your luck's in, Alec. We've got Scotland Yard on the job now.'

'Scotland Yard—?'

'George Gently in person.'

The brown eyes stared at Gently in alarm. 'But—!'

'We were all at his place when the news came

14

through and Sir Tommy collared him straight away.'

'You mean . . .?'

'He'll be running the show now. So you can sit back and relax, old fellow.'

But Beresford didn't look very relaxed.

'Right, then,' Sir Tommy barked. 'If we've got that sorted, perhaps we can get down to business. A little more detail is what we want—just what did happen here last night. Who is going to be first?'

'But—' Beresford faltered.

'Come on, come on!' Sir Tommy said. 'What happened out there was no accident. Something triggered it and we need to know what. Can none of you people put a finger on it?'

Beresford and his wife exchanged anguished looks.

'But everything was so normal!' Melanie Beresford said. 'In fact, it was one of our best evenings. The play, everything. It went so well.'

'I was going to say the same,' Beresford said. 'It was perhaps our most successful soirée ever. Our poor young protégé had just been published and Paul's play was chosen for the Little Theatre. Success was in the air and people were responding to it.'

'It was a *happy* evening,' Melanie Beresford said. 'Ambrose was popular and everyone was glad for him. And that includes even you, Lesley.'

15

'Don't pick on me, Mother!' The young man flushed.

'Our son is a poet too,' Melanie Beresford said. 'So far, he hasn't been very lucky. But that didn't stop him congratulating Ambrose.'

'Well . . .!'

'I heard you, Lesley. And it was the same with everyone else. Whoever did this dreadful thing, it wasn't anyone who was at the soirée.'

Lesley Beresford hung his head.

'And that goes for me too, Sir Thomas,' Beresford said. 'It couldn't have been any of our lot who did it. That simply is beyond all credibility.'

Sir Tommy fixed him with a gaze. 'What about that painter fellow I heard tell of?'

'Who—?'

'The painter fellow. The one with the girl-friend whom young Keats was making up to?'

'He means Christopher,' Melanie Beresford said. 'But that is quite, quite, ridiculous.'

'Christopher?'

'I don't think he liked Liz and Ambrose making love in the play. But to suggest because of that! They weren't even acting, just reading the parts. And Liz was deliberately playing it down, there was nothing he could take exception to.'

Sir Tommy said: 'But didn't he clear out?'

'If he did, I didn't notice.'

'I'm afraid he did,' Reymerston said. 'He collected his gear together and hooked it.'

16

'Well, it didn't have to be because of that!' Melanie Beresford said. 'He could have had a dozen reasons for leaving early. But even if it was, can you seriously imagine him doing anything so frightful?'

Slowly, Reymerston shook his head.

'I noticed he wasn't there at the end,' Beresford admitted. 'But I have to agree, he's the last person . . .'

'Of course he is, Alec.'

Sir Tommy stared from one to the other. 'Now listen,' he said. 'These things can happen. We're looking for motive and opportunity, and this painter fellow seems to have had both. I can understand your wanting to be loyal but what we're dealing with is homicide and facts we cannot overlook. Was he the only one to leave early?'

'I believe . . .' Beresford jiffled his shoulders. 'You see, it's difficult, Sir Thomas! We have about thirty of them here and you can't keep an eye on everyone. After the play-reading we had coffee and as far as I know they were all present, but I couldn't swear to it. They break up in groups and some leave at once, others hang on a little.'

'But before that?'

Beresford shook his head.

'And you, madam?'

'I'm sorry, Sir Thomas.'

Sir Tommy looked at Reymerston, who sighed. 'Just one thing,' he said. 'Ambrose was among the first to leave. He left his coffee half-drunk, grabbed his briefcase and went. But that's all.'

'He left alone?'

'I can't tell you that. A few of the others had just gone and he may have caught up with them.'

'Were there blokes among them?'

'Very likely. But I didn't particularly notice.'

'And he was in a hurry to get after them?'

'It's possible. You could say that.'

'Look, this is crazy!' Beresford broke in. 'It was just another of our sessions breaking up. You really can't read more into it than that, what happened out there must have taken place later.'

'Fellow died about then,' Sir Tommy said. 'The doctor puts it before midnight.'

'So. We broke up at half-past ten.'

Sir Tommy shook his head. 'Puts it right in the bracket.'

'But!' Beresford stared helplessly. 'Look, it just isn't making sense! If there'd been a row people would have noticed and he couldn't have been dragged in there without one. It could have been something quite different. He could have spotted an intruder and gone in after him. There have been some break-ins around here lately and this place would be a prime target.'

Sir Tommy gazed at him. 'Nice try,' he said.

'But it does make more sense!'

18

'We'll look at it,' Sir Tommy said. 'We'll look at everything. But a gung-ho burglar is way down the list.' He sighed and looked round for Gently. 'Any comments from the maestro?' he said.

Gently shrugged. 'Perhaps a query.' His glance strayed to the couple and their son. 'When people were leaving, would one or other of you have been in the porch, bidding them goodbye?'

'Aha!' Sir Tommy said.

'Well, I wasn't,' Beresford said. 'I was chatting to people in here. Did you go out, Melanie?'

'No, I stayed here too. But—' Melanie Beresford checked herself.

'Lesley?' Beresford said.

'Yes ... I thought ...'

Lesley Beresford stared hard but said nothing.

* * *

'All right then—I was out there! But I don't have anything to tell you.'

Lesley Beresford was a lean-built young man with sharp features that favoured his mother. He blushed easily and was blushing now as he felt all their eyes upon him. He dug his hands in his pockets. He wasn't much over twenty. He was dressed in a multi-coloured shirt, denims and trainers.

19

Gently said: 'Were you there when Ambrose West left?'

'Yes—I may have been. I don't know! I was probably talking to some of the others. Yes, I may have seen him go by.'

'He was in a hurry?'

'Yes—I think.'

'And he was alone?'

'Yes—alone!'

Gently paused. 'You are quite sure of that?'

'I tell you yes—I'm quite sure!'

'Could he have been hurrying to catch someone up?'

Lesley Beresford dug his hands deeper in his pockets.

'Do tell them what you know,' Melanie Beresford said. 'It probably isn't important, but it could help them.'

'Mother—please!'

'She's right,' Beresford said. 'They'll probably find out anyway from other people.'

'Oh lord!'

Hot-faced, he stared at the carpet, his lips pressed tight.

Gently said: 'He was pursuing someone. Could it have been a young lady?'

'Oh, not Liz!' Melanie Beresford exclaimed. 'Do tell us it wasn't Liz, Lesley.'

'I won't—I'm not going to tell anything!'

'But you must, Lesley. You must!'

'Why should I?'

'Then it was Liz!'

20

'I haven't said so—'

'You don't have to.'

She stared at her husband in dismay: Beresford's hands were working again. He drew a deep breath. 'Bloody tell them, Lesley,' he said.

'But—why should I?'

'Just tell them.'

'You're not going to like this—'

'Tell them!'

The young man was trembling. 'All right then—it was Liz! She left on her own and he ran after her. I couldn't hear what was said. But then he took her by the arm and she went with him. Into the shrubbery.'

'They went there—!'

'Yes. And now you know all I can tell you. I came in, I didn't hang about, it made me feel sick. I just came in.'

Sir Tommy gazed at Gently. 'Well, well!'

Gently said: 'Would anyone else have seen this?'

'No. There was just us.'

'And the lady went willingly?'

'Yes . . . I think so.'

'And—you saw no one else at all?'

He shook his head at the carpet.

'Good lad!' Sir Tommy said. 'I don't know, George, but I'm beginning to think we may have this business wrapped up. What do you say?'

But Gently only shrugged. 'First, we'd better

21

talk to the girl,' he said.

'Oh, everything by the book,' Sir Tommy said. 'But I may not have to ring Gilly after all. Eykey can take this young man's statement, and the girl we'll have down at the station. Then we'll see. We may just have our man in a cell tonight.'

'I suppose—' Beresford began.

'Don't worry, old man! We'll keep it under wraps as far as we can.'

Beresford shook his head. 'I don't know,' he said. 'But I simply can't believe it, even now. There must be some other explanation. It's all a nightmare that shouldn't be happening.'

And Reymerston was staring hard at Gently.

'Right,' Sir Tommy said. 'What's the name of this girl?'

CHAPTER TWO

Eyke was saddled with the routine work, the statements, lists, the apprehending of the girl. Her full name was Elizabeth Simpson, Beresford told them, and she lived with her parents in a bungalow by the common. A girl with ambitions. She worked at a dress shop, but her heart was on the stage and for two seasons now she had played minor roles in the town's Little Theatre. She had the looks, she had the figure and Derek Hopkins, the producer, thought she might go far.

22

'And this painter fellow was her steady?'

Beresford had tried to play it down, but his wife was unable to conceal her opinion. No question: Chris Clarke was the man in her life.

'I don't know, George!'

They had left Eyke to it and drifted the Jag back into town. Sir Tommy had selected the Pelican and now they sat in the bar with pints in front of them. Sir Tommy had a frown on his furrowed brow. It was some moments before he lifted his glass. Now he sighed, took a pull, set the glass back down and stared at it.

'What do you think of it? Those bloody people? Would you say any of them were quite normal? I mean, the way they carry on, their stupid meetings, the whole palaver? I wouldn't! I'd say it was asking for it, getting together a crowd like that. Sooner or later there was bound to be trouble and Alec has only himself to blame.'

'Beresford could scarcely have foreseen this.'

Sir Tommy snorted. 'You're trying to be kind! But he is as bad as the rest, or worse. And don't forget he's Janet's cousin.'

Gently drank. 'He could just have a point.'

'How do you mean?'

'The culprit could be an outsider.'

Sir Tommy stared, then shook his head. 'It doesn't add up, George. It simply doesn't. I mean, just look at the facts. That fellow was battered in Alec's garden. He was canoodling

23

there with another bloke's woman, and the bloke knew about it and was out there waiting for them.'

Gently said: 'We don't know that yet.'

'Oh, come on!' Sir Tommy said. 'He saw what was going on back there and cleared off to catch them when they came out. Nothing else makes sense and you know it. Bloody Alec was just catching at straws.'

'But . . . would he have responded quite so violently?'

'It happens. And we're dealing with off-beats.'

'And yet no disturbance was reported.'

'That may come. When we talk to the others.'

They drank. It was early and they had the bar almost to themselves. The windows gave on the High Street, across which, nearly opposite, was a dress shop, perhaps the one where Elizabeth Simpson was employed. But this was Sunday. Among numerous strollers, only one or two paused before the shop. Suddenly, watching them, Gently felt again the sense of fatigue he had experienced earlier. Perhaps he would be glad to duck out of this one! After all, wasn't the rest likely to be just routine . . .?

Sir Tommy glanced at his watch. 'They're taking their time!'

Eyke had been briefed to advise them when the girl was fetched.

'You don't think she's hopped it?'

24

'She may not have been at home.'

'On the other hand . . . if she was a witness!'

Gently drank. They had only been there twenty minutes. At best, they might expect a wait of half an hour. He filled a pipe and lit it. Sir Tommy watched him impatiently, then drained his glass.

'I think we'll get over there, George. If there are problems we need to be on the spot.'

'Eyke won't let us down.'

'All the same. We ought to be there when they bring her in.'

Gently sighed and reached for his glass. Outside, a patrol-car had just gone by. And, as they rose from their table, the swing doors of the bar opened to reveal Eyke.

'Eykey! Have you got her?'

Eykey had. They were fetching her in at that very moment.

* * *

'She's in a bit of a state I'm afraid, sir. She nearly flipped when she heard why we wanted her.'

It was only a short distance to the police station and Sir Tommy had left the Jag parked at the Pelican.

'We had to help her into the car and her parents, they were carrying on too. He's the clerk to some solicitor. We'll probably have him on our necks.'

25

'Girl's a blasted actress, isn't she?'

'Don't think she was acting just now, sir. It really hit her. She collapsed on a chair and went as white as two sheets.'

'Could be the shock of finding we had a line on her.'

'Well, it could have been, sir.' But Eyke didn't sound convinced.

In reception they were met by Eyke's sidekick, Metfield, who also wore an expression of concern.

'She's in your office, chief. I thought it best. I've got WPC Jones along with her.'

'Tell Sarah we'll need her too.'

'She's standing by all ready, chief.'

They entered the office. On a chair by the desk sat a dark, slender girl in her midtwenties. She sat slumped, her eyes staring, her hands grasping a handkerchief on her lap. Beside her sat a WPC, who rose as they came in.

'Find another chair, Eykey.'

Sir Tommy took the one behind the desk himself. He peered curiously at the girl, who seemed not to have noticed their incursion. Her pallid cheeks were wet. She was twisting the handkerchief between her hands. She had large, green eyes, which were directed at the front of the desk, but clearly unaware of it: they were seeing something else. Her hair, worn medium-length, enclosed fine, symmetrical features and she was wearing a simple green

26

dress that suggested a shapely figure.

They were joined by a second WPC carrying a shorthand pad and pencil. She took her seat at the end of the desk: Gently had chosen a chair at the other end. Sir Tommy eased himself back in his seat.

'So . . . it's Miss Elizabeth Simpson, is it?'

For a moment she continued to stare, then her eyes flickered into focus. She gazed fearfully at Sir Tommy.

'I suppose we know why we're here, do we? We've come to help sort out this bad business? To put the culprit where he belongs?'

'But . . . I've told them already!'

'You've told them what, my dear?'

'I—!' She burst suddenly into tears. 'It isn't true—no, it can't be! Tell me. Tell me it isn't true!'

Sir Tommy shook his head. 'It's no use carrying on, my girl. What's done is done and your putting on an act isn't going to help.'

'Ambrose isn't dead!'

'You'll just have to face it.'

'I can't, I won't believe that!'

Sir Tommy sat up straighter. 'Now listen,' he said. 'This sort of behaviour is getting us nowhere.'

'But it isn't true!'

'Yes it damn-well is. They carted the fellow off an hour ago.'

'No. Not Ambrose!'

'Well, it wasn't his double. And I suppose the

27

Beresfords were capable of identifying him.'

'I won't believe it—I can't!'

'Oh hell,' Sir Tommy said. 'You talk to her, George!'

Gently regarded the sobbing girl for a moment. 'Perhaps we could have a coffee-break,' he said. 'A little time for things to settle.'

Sir Tommy glared at Eyke. 'Do what the man says!'

The coffee was fetched. Miss Simpson sobbed on. But now the sobs were becoming less frequent. In the end WPC Jones, a kindly-faced woman, persuaded her to take a sip from her mug. Then she dabbed her eyes, sought to pull herself together and fixed the reddened eyes on the desk. Gently took a sip from his own mug.

'You would know the Beresfords very well, Miss Simpson.'

'Yes. Yes, of course!'

'They too are very much upset. It was an especial shock for Alec Beresford.'

'You mean—?' At last her eyes met his.

Gently nodded. 'I'm afraid so.'

'Then . . .?'

'Regrettably, yes. However tragic, it has to be accepted.'

She gulped and sat very still.

'He will be a loss,' Gently said. 'He was an asset to your circle. My wife and I met him in the bookshop. He seemed a very likeable

28

young man. We shall be questioning not only yourself to discover how this thing could happen to him. I'm sure you will understand that and give us all the help you can.'

'But . . .' Something flickered in her eye.

'Perhaps we should start at the beginning of the evening?'

'The beginning . . .?'

'Just in case you remember something that could be of importance to us.'

Her stare was wild for a moment, then she shook her head. 'No . . . there was nothing!'

'Think about it. The young man had brought copies of the book he had just published. He was signing them for people. Does that suggest anything to you?'

'No. Nothing.'

'Did you buy one from him?'

'He—actually, he gave me one.'

'So he was giving them to his friends?'

She twisted the handkerchief. 'Well . . . he gave one to me!'

'Just . . . to you?'

'I don't know!'

'Not, for example, to your friend Christopher Clarke?'

'To Chris!' Her eyes jumped wide and the hands twisting the handkerchief froze.

Gently said: 'Andy Reymerston was with us earlier, before we heard what had happened to poor young West. He was giving us an account of the evening, of the play-reading and the rest.

29

You took a part in the reading, he told us.'

'So—if I did?'

'You were playing opposite West. There was a love scene involved, to which your friend Chris appeared to take exception. In fact at that point, according to Andy, he packed up and left. Can you confirm that?'

There was horror in her eyes. 'Listen, you can't—!'

'But can you confirm it?'

'No!'

'You were unaware that he had gone?'

Her hands dragged on the handkerchief. 'I was reading my part, that's all! I don't know when he went. It couldn't have been to do with me.'

'Not because of the part you were playing.'

'That's ... ridiculous! Chris knew it didn't mean a thing.'

'He had no cause for jealousy.'

'No, of course not!'

'There was nothing between you and West?'

'Oh God, no!'

'Not even an appearance of it?'

She burst into tears and covered her face.

'Come on now,' Sir Tommy said. 'You'll do well to admit to it, old girl. He was a handsome young fellow and he'd got it going for him. No one's going to blame you for giving him a whirl.'

'But it wasn't anything!'

'Painter fellow thought it was.'

30

'He didn't—he couldn't. You don't understand!'

'He slung his hook, though.'

'I can't help it! Chris knew there was nothing to it. He knew that for me there was only him, however much Ambrose hung around me.'

'So—did he hang around?'

'Yes—yes!'

'But he wasn't getting anywhere?'

'Oh God!'

'Not even—last night?'

'No. No!'

'When the show broke up?'

She could only sob.

Gently said: 'We have certain testimony, Miss Simpson, about what occurred when people were leaving. It seems to suggest that something passed between West and yourself at that time. Perhaps, when you feel able, you can give us your account of what happened.'

Her sobs only increased. The WPC slid a sympathetic arm round her. Elizabeth Simpson buried her face in the woman's chest and sobbed uncontrollably.

Gently sipped some cold coffee and felt for his pipe. But didn't light it.

Sir Tommy cradled his chin in his hands and gazed at the weeping woman, a gleam in his eye. Then at Gently.

Meanwhile, the shorthand-writer took the opportunity to sharpen a pencil.

'It wasn't what you think!'

31

Elizabeth Simpson jerked herself away from the WPC. Her face was a mess. She scrubbed at it with a handkerchief already sodden with tears.

Gently said: 'I believe you set off from the house on your own.'

'Yes I did—and do you want to know why? It was because I was trying to avoid him. To avoid Ambrose!' She scrubbed desperately. 'It's true, then! I did see Chris leave. And the look he gave me, even though he knew . . . and I was trying so hard to show him it all meant nothing!'

'West was paying you attention.'

'Yes. Yes! Oh, I should have given him the push sooner. It was just a game, a bit of a joke. He knew he would never get me away from Chris. But then that stupid play . . . I had to read lines that nearly choked me.'

'Lines in which you were declaring love.'

'Yes. I did my best to read them flat. But Ambrose didn't. He was giving them everything. You could easily believe he really meant them. And then I caught Chris's eye, and the next moment he jumped up and went to fetch his things . . .' She sniffled. 'I wanted to run after him, but I couldn't very well break up the play. So I had to let him go. And perhaps I was a little miffed to feel that he didn't trust me.'

'About when would this have been?'

'How should I know! It may have been eight

32

or thereabouts.'

'And the meeting went on until ten-thirty?'

'Yes, about then. That was usual.'

Gently nodded. 'So the play continued.'

'We were only in the first act. And afterwards there was a discussion, and then coffee and refreshments. Ambrose kept trying to get me to himself, but I wasn't having any of that. I stuck close to Melanie and Derek Hopkins, who is putting on the play at the Little. In the end, when we broke up, I waited till I thought Ambrose was occupied signing one of his books, then I sneaked out smartly. Only, it wasn't smartly enough.'

'He followed you and caught you up.'

She twisted the handkerchief. 'Who was it saw us?'

Gently shrugged. 'It doesn't matter!'

'How much did they see?'

He shook his head.

Elizabeth Simpson's mouth clamped tight and she stared at the tormented handkerchief. Fear and indecision were in that gaze, and also a trace of bafflement. Her shoulder moved.

'All right then! Since you seem to know all about it. Yes, he did chase after me, and yes, I was fool enough to do what he asked.'

'What was it he wanted?'

'Do I have to tell you? He was after a session in the shrubbery. People have always gone in there to snog, it's one of the traditions of the soirées.'

33

'And you agreed to his invitation?'

She almost spat it out. 'Yes!'

'Even though you had been trying to avoid him?'

'Because of that. Don't you see?' Her wretched eyes sought Gently's. 'I wanted to have it out, once and for all. It had gone too far, it was upsetting Chris, it was time to tell Ambrose where he got off.'

'And that was why you went with him?'

'Don't you believe me?'

'Did you have to go in there to talk to him?'

'Yes—we could have been interrupted! And I didn't want to show him up in front of the others.' The tears were welling again in her eyes. 'Can't you understand? Ambrose wasn't a bad sort. I was trying not to hurt him, but it had to be done. I just wasn't for him, that's all.'

Gently nodded. 'So you accompanied him in there.'

She dabbed her eyes. 'Yes.'

'What happened?'

'He—tried to make love to me and I shoved him away. And told him.'

'How did he take it?'

She fought down a sob. 'Badly. He—he didn't want to believe me. He kept trying to take me in his arms and in the end . . .' She hung her head. 'I slapped his face. And ran.'

'You—ran.'

'Yes. I wanted out.'

'And he didn't follow you?'

34

She shook her head. 'He was shocked, I think. I left him standing there, feeling his face. He didn't come after me.'

'And then—you went home?'

'Yes. It was all over in a couple of minutes. I caught up with some other girls who were leaving and kept with them. Just in case.'

'Do you remember who they were?'

'I can give you their names! Sue Wilcox, Cathy Bennett and Sarah Wright. I walked with them up into the town, then we split up and went our own ways.'

'And—West you left in the shrubbery.'

'Oh, my God!' She collapsed again into sobs.

Gently said: 'I must ask you this. Were you and West alone there in the shrubbery?'

She gasped. 'Yes . . . yes! Who else could there have been there?'

'I'm asking you.'

'No, there was no one!'

'You formed no impression of being watched?'

'No—please! I saw no one.'

'Perhaps, when you ran off?'

Her tears came in storms.

Sir Tommy gave one of his snorts. 'Now listen here, girl! You aren't quite a fool. Young West didn't bash his own head in and we know of someone who might have done it for him.'

She howled.

'Did you see him, or not?'

'It isn't true—you can't think—!'

'Got it in for him, hadn't he, your painter fellow, and took off early from the binge?'

'Chris!' She stared, open-mouthed.

'Stands out a mile,' Sir Tommy said.

But still Elizabeth Simpson was staring at him as though she couldn't believe her ears.

'You can't—you can't—!'

'Come on, old girl! No use your trying to protect him. He'll get off light in the circs, around six years if I know anything.'

'But you simply can't!—'

'Make it easy for yourself.'

In desperation she turned to Gently. 'You don't believe this—that Chris . . .?'

'No one else in the picture,' Sir Tommy said.

She stared in complete shock, her body stiff, her hands motionless. Then she gave the howl again and her hands wrenched apart.

'It isn't fair—you can't do this! Chris would never have hurt Ambrose. Why don't you blame me? I was there, I could have done it!'

Sir Tommy clicked his tongue. 'Talk sense, old girl! It took a better man than you.'

'But not Chris. You just don't know him. You'll be making a terrible mistake.'

'Well, we shall see about that.'

'No!'

'We can't just let it ride, my dear.'

'It wasn't him. He didn't do it!'

Sir Tommy sighed and rolled his eyes.

Gently said: 'You are quite certain—you saw

36

no other person when you were in the shrubbery?'

'Please . . . no!'

'Or in that neighbourhood—the sweep, the drive. Perhaps in the porch?'

She shook her head desperately. 'You must believe me!'

'You can add nothing else at all?'

'I swear it—nothing. It was just us. And then the girls I told you about.'

Gently nodded. 'And since last night would you have been in touch with Clarke?'

'With Chris—no! After his behaviour, I thought I would let him stew. He had shown everyone he didn't trust me and it was up to him to make the first move.'

'It had been very public.'

'Everyone saw it. Some of the bitches were giggling and nudging each other. I saw Melanie whisper something to Alec, and Lesley heard it and gave us a queer look.'

'A queer look . . .?'

'You know. As though he were wondering if it was serious.'

Gently shrugged and looked at Sir Tommy.

'Well . . . that's about it, my dear,' Sir Tommy said. 'We will need to have a signed statement from you, but that's all.' He stared hard at her. 'Unless you have anything you would like to add.'

'No, I've told you everything! But . . .'

'But?'

37

She stared at her hands. 'I still can't believe it! Or that you should think for one moment . . .' She was struggling to keep back a fresh bout of sobs. 'You're not going to arrest him, are you?'

'Got to have a talk with him, old girl.'

'Yes, but . . .!'

Sir Tommy hesitated. 'Sure there's nothing else you want to tell us?'

Was there?

Elizabeth Simpson seemed in the grip of some impossible dilemma, her hands grappling with the handkerchief, her eyes averted, lips trembling. But in the end she got it out: 'No . . . no. Nothing else!'

* * *

'The lying bitch!'

The office had been cleared of everyone but themselves and Eyke. Sir Tommy had lit a cigar, Gently his pipe. Eyke was contenting himself with cold coffee. For a while, after she had been escorted out, there was silence: then Sir Tommy delivered his judgement.

'You think she does know something, sir?'

'Damned certain she does. She's covering for the fellow all the way. She could put him on the spot for us, Eykey, that's what the snivelling was all about.'

'You mean she could have seen what happened, sir.'

38

Sir Tommy drilled smoke. 'Could have done. But more likely she took off before he laid into the young Shelley and Keats.'

'He would have been waiting outside for them, sir.'

'Right. He was hanging about out there. Then he saw the pair of them go into the shrubbery and went right in after them.'

'Could have caught them at it.'

'What else? And the girl hooks it as fast as she can. Then chummie pulls out a stake and whacks the young man, and scarpers too. That's the picture we're faced with, Eykey, and the one that's going to impress a jury. And if the girl-friend won't come across, we'll just have to fit chummie without her assistance.'

'Shouldn't be too hard, sir.'

Sir Tommy nodded. 'Not with the set-up the way it is.' He breathed smoke in Gently's direction. 'Any comments from you, George?'

Gently shrugged. 'Only this. They must all have been very quiet about it. Those three girls were leaving about then and surely must have heard any row that was in progress.'

Sir Tommy frowned. 'Needn't have been a row. Chummie just sails in there and gets to business. Girl sees him coming and sneaks out, then chummie lets fly without a word being spoken.'

Gently shook his head. 'It's difficult to picture . . .'

'Perhaps the girls did hear something, sir,'

39

Eyke said. 'They could have ignored it, they weren't to know. And we'll be talking to them anyway.'

'There you are, then,' Sir Tommy said. 'Three more nails for his coffin. Are you with me now?'

Gently blew a smoke-ring. 'One thing I didn't see fit to ask Miss Simpson,' he said. 'But, before we descend on Clarke, it might be useful to know what clothes he was wearing last night.'

'By golly, yes!'

'Just in case.'

'Get me Alec on the phone,' Sir Tommy said. 'If he doesn't know, his wife will. You can depend on the ladies for that.'

The information was noted: Clarke had been dressed in a claret sports-shirt, cotton slacks and a lightweight anorak, and shod in either trainers or plimsolls, Melanie Beresford couldn't remember which. The slacks were cream-coloured, the anorak beige and the shirt had a device embroidered on the breast-pocket. Eyke jotted it down as Sir Tommy repeated it.

'Right,' the latter said, hanging up. `Now we're ready for the bloke. Detail a couple of men, Eykey, and you come with us to show us where he lives.'

'Do you think he'll give trouble, sir?'

'Better hadn't,' Sir Tommy said. 'But there's no harm in going prepared. What do you say,

40

George?'

But Gently merely knocked out his pipe, rose and made to follow them.

CHAPTER THREE

The Jag preceded the patrol-car. Eyke directed them back by the green and the Beresford house. There, having reached a level, the road pursued its course towards the river and harbour, bounded on one side by beach and sea, on the other by ranging marshes; with, on the landward side, a ribbon of beleaguered-seeming properties. Clearly, it was flood territory: sandbags were stacked beside a few of the entries. A dyke separated the properties from the marshes, low marram banks from the sea: bungalows, two doubtful houses and, down by the harbour, a low-lying camp-site.

'This is it, sir.'

Sir Tommy grunted and drifted the Jag in beside one of the properties. A timber bungalow of uncertain age, it stood only a yard or two clear of the road. Through the open door of an adjacent garage one could see the rear-end of a Lada estate-car, and beyond it a rough lawn, terminating abruptly at the dyke. Access to the dwelling was a stable door, of which the top half yawned wide. As they got out a man appeared there: a man clad in a claret-coloured sports-shirt.

41

'Christopher Clarke?'

'That's my name.'

'Suppose you know why we're here, Clarke?'

'Oh yes!'

He glared at Sir Tommy, then at the patrol-car and its uniformed crew: a man in his early thirties, of powerful build, strong-featured, his chin jutting.

'Expecting us, were you?'

'I was told to!'

'Were you now. And who by?'

'Does it matter who it was?'

'I', Sir Tommy said, 'wouldn't take that tone.'

Christopher Clarke's chin jutted some more. 'Let's say by a friend, shall we?' he said. 'A friend who knows how the official mind works, who wanted to warn me what to expect. Is that good enough?'

'I want a name, my lad.'

'Then you know what you can do.'

'This isn't going to help you, Clarke.'

'So that's my bloody bad luck, isn't it?'

Now they were both glaring at each other. Gently moved up hastily in Sir Tommy's rear. 'Perhaps we should go inside,' he said. 'We can discuss it better there.'

'I don't want to discuss it!'

'All the same. And wouldn't it be Andy who gave you the news?'

Christopher Clarke's eyes switched to Gently. 'You!' he said. 'Are you him?'

'I expect Andy mentioned me.'

'Yes . . . he did! And he said . . . but never mind!'

Sir Tommy gave a snort of disgust. 'Damned fellow briefed you, did he?' he said. 'I suppose one should have expected it—another dauber like yourself! But don't think it's going to help you, Clarke. We've got some questions that need answers. So you can just drop the front and try a little co-operation.'

'Oh yes?' His look was bitter. 'And where is that supposed to get me?'

Sir Tommy eyed him. 'If you want an opinion . . .' He shrugged. 'We'll come to that later! For now, just open this door.'

'And if I refuse?'

'Then I'll have you arrested.'

Christopher Clarke's mouth twisted. He looked at Gently, Eyke, and the two uniform-men. And finally unbolted the lower half of the door.

* * *

It gave directly into a small lounge furnished, not unattractively, in the period of the Thirties, with the addition of a modem stove in the chimney-piece and a music-centre in one corner. Among pictures hung on the walls Gently recognised one of Reymerston's, a pointillist experiment; along with a series of beachscapes, each signed with a firm C. The

43

room was scrupulously tidy. On the lino-clad floor lay variegated rag-mats, on a bamboo table a bowl of dried flowers.

Clarke retired to the end of the room and took a defiant stand before the stove. The shirt he was wearing was clearly that of yesterday, but the slacks had been exchanged for jeans. Also, today he wore sandals, an open pattern that exposed his bare feet. Sir Tommy regarded him with narrowed eyes.

'Right then, Clarke! We'll get to business. I don't have to tell you what happened last night, after that affair broke up at Beresford's. Just to put you in the picture, we've talked to Miss Simpson, who admitted her part in the incident. So now we come to you and what you can tell us about it. Are you going to come clean?'

'You've—talked to Liz?'

'Oh yes, my lad.'

'But—what can she have had to do with it?'

Sir Tommy fixed him with his stare. 'Don't waste our time acting the innocent! She's your girl and West was after her, and you couldn't bear to watch it going on. You took off from Beresford's in a paddy and there's a dozen or two witnesses to prove it. And young West finishes up bashed in the shrubbery. Are you going to tell us it was some coincidence?'

Clarke's eyes were wide. 'But that was afterwards—after Liz had gone home! She couldn't have played any part in that.'

44

'Is that a fact,' Sir Tommy said. 'Are you going to give us your word on it?'

'How—how do you mean?'

'I mean this. Either she saw it happen or she didn't. According to her she cleared out of the shrubbery before the attack on West took place. And you are telling us that's a fact?'

Clarke's mouth gaped. 'And she—Liz—was in the shrubbery?'

'Of course she bloody was! Along with West. They went there together.'

'But Andy didn't say—'

'Wanted to spare your feelings, did he?'

'Oh no!'

'Come on,' Sir Tommy said. 'You're not kidding anyone with an act like that. The girl swears she cleared out before it happened, so you may as well back her up. Says she didn't see you either, for what it's going to be worth.'

'But . . . she was there.'

Gently said: 'If it helps, she went there to have a show-down with West. She was upset when you left early and wanted to make it clear to West that he stood no chance with her.'

'Oh lord . . . what a mess!'

'Needn't have bashed him,' Sir Tommy said.

Clarke threw himself down on a chair, sat staring at one of the rag-mats.

Gently said: 'Have you anything to tell us?'

'Oh, what's the use!' Clarke groaned. 'The way it is I must have done it, nobody will ever believe any different.'

'Are you admitting you did?'

'Does it matter?'

'I would advise you to give it a little thought.'

'A little thought!' He kicked at the mat. 'Is that going to stop you from arresting me? If I'd found them together there . . . I don't know! I might have done what you say!'

'You . . . might have done?'

'I don't know! But it's what everyone is going to think.'

'But . . . did you?'

Clarke stared, and gave the mat a vicious kick.

Gently said: 'Let us go back to the meeting. West was celebrating his success. He was signing copies of his book for people and made a point of presenting one to Miss Simpson. No doubt you took exception to his attitude. Did any incident arise from that?'

'No, it bloody didn't!'

Gently nodded. 'Then he and Miss Simpson were given parts in the play. It involved a scene in which they made love and in which, she tells us, he played his part with obvious enthusiasm. Apparently you found this intolerable and abruptly withdrew from the proceedings. Is that correct?'

Clarke glared at him. 'So if I did?'

Gently said: 'From that point we have no information. So what we require now is a statement of your movements. Where you went. Whom you met. Where you were when

46

that meeting broke up.'

'But—what's the sodding use?'

'You prefer not to tell us?'

Clarke's stare returned to the misused mat. 'You're not going to believe me if I do. You've made your minds up about me already.'

'We still need your statement.'

He kicked the mat. 'All bloody right then, for what it's worth! I spent the rest of last night in a pub, trying to forget what had been going on.'

'In a pub . . . ?'

'Now call me a liar. And after the pub turned out, I came home.'

* * *

'And—what was the name of this lousy pub?'

Sir Tommy hadn't exactly called Clarke a liar. But the tone of his voice and his narrowed eyes left no doubt of his opinion.

'I don't remember its name—'

'Ha!'

Clarke groaned. 'Is there any use in my trying to tell you? It was a pub I had never been in before, so probably no one is going to remember me.'

'Carry on, my lad.'

'Oh hell!' He turned an appealing look on Gently. 'I wanted to get away, as far as I could. You can understand that, can't you?'

Gently solemnly nodded.

'I went up through the town. All the way.

47

Across the bridge. There's a pub out there at the junction, where a road turns off up the coast. I hadn't meant to go in there, but that's what I did. And I took my drink to a bench outside. The place was crowded and I didn't want company; I just sat outside in the garden.'

Gently said: 'A pub at the junction . . .?'

Eyke said: 'The Brewer's Arms, sir. I sometimes drop in there myself.'

'The Brewer's Arms . . .'

'They do a good meal there. The publican's name is Jeff Stringer.'

Gently said: 'And you spoke to nobody?'

'No, I told you!' Clarke lunged at the mat. 'I didn't know anyone and I wasn't in the mood. I just bought my drink and went outside.'

'Was there no one else out there?'

'Yes . . . perhaps. I remember a couple who came out. But they weren't interested in me, they went to a bench on the other side. Then there was a bloke with a dog, but that's all. The crowd was inside.'

'Who served you at the counter?'

'Some girl . . .'

'How many drinks did you buy?'

'A couple of pints.'

'Was anything going on there that you remember?'

He stared for a moment, but shook his head.

'And . . . you stayed there till closing, I think you said.'

'Yes . . .' Had he hesitated, just a fraction?

48

'Till half-past ten . . . it could have been later. It was well after eleven when I got back here.'

'You would have passed Mr Beresford's house.'

He merely nodded.

'You met none of your friends leaving?'

'No. They would all have gone by then. I tell you, it was after eleven.'

'You are sure of that?'

'Yes, I'm sure! I had a mile to walk back from the pub.'

Sir Tommy snorted his disbelief. 'It's a good tale, my lad!' he said. 'Just a damned shame you can't prove it. Such a pity that you weren't in the mood for chat. You don't want to change anything?'

'No! Why should I?'

'Thought I'd give you the chance,' Sir Tommy said. 'You certainly need it. But if that's the story, all we need now is to put it on paper. Oh, and just one other thing. Where are those slacks you were wearing last night?'

'My slacks?'

Sir Tommy nodded. 'And the trainers. Or were they plimsolls?'

Clarke's eyes were large. 'And you really think—!'

'Don't make us hunt for them, old son. Life is hard enough already.'

For an instant Clarke sat staring at him, then he sprang up from the chair. 'Right,' he said. 'Right! If that's the idea, just follow me.'

He threw open a door into a hall and led them to a door lower down. It gave access to a bedroom with windows looking out on the scruffy lawn. A double-doored wardrobe stood in one comer. Clarke slammed the doors apart. From among clothes suspended on hangers from the rails inside he pulled out a pair of slacks and threw them on the bed, then followed them with an anorak and a pair of trainers taken from the bottom of the wardrobe. The slacks were cream-coloured, the anorak of a hue that might be described as beige. Clarke was breathing hard.

'So there you bloody are! See what you can find out from them. And this was the shirt I was wearing, and those are the socks on that chair.'

Eyke spread out the slacks eagerly and Sir Tommy chivvied the anorak. One thing seemed plain: neither garment gave any indication of having lately been washed. Neither were there any obvious signs of spongeing or other attempts at cleansing. Frowning, Sir Tommy passed on to the trainers, then to the socks hanging over the chair.

'Take a look through the wardrobe, Eykey!'

Eyke did as he was bid. But no alternatives were available to the garments Clarke had produced. The painter was watching them with a glint in his eye.

'Perhaps you are satisfied now?'

'Oh no!' Sir Tommy said. 'We don't give up so easily, laddie. This lot is going to forensic,

50

and if you've tried to be clever we'll' soon know about that. Also, I'll have that shirt you've got on.'

'My sodding shirt—'

'Let's be having it.'

Momentarily it seemed that Clarke might defy him, but then he wrenched the shirt off and tossed it on the bed. He took another from a drawer and savagely pulled it over his head.

'So that's it? You're arresting me?'

Sir Tommy eyed him. 'Just pulling you in, sonny. You're going to give us your signed statement and then sit tight while we make some enquiries.'

'It's the same bloody thing!'

Gently said: 'Not quite. Just now you are assisting our investigation. If our enquiries support your account there will be no reason to detain you.'

'If,' Sir Tommy said. 'If!'

Clarke glared at him, but was silent. Meanwhile Eyke had located a bin-bag, into which he stuffed the suspect clothing.

'Right,' Sir Tommy said.

And they marched Clarke out to the cars.

* * *

The clothes were despatched post-haste to forensic and Eyke's sergeant, Campsey, to the Brewer's Arms. In their absence two of the girls mentioned by Miss Simpson had been located and had given accounts that confirmed her own. Yes, she had run after them as they were leaving and had walked back with them into the town. She had seemed a little breathless and upset, but had said nothing that might account for it. One of the girls had ribbed her about a certain person and had received a biting riposte.

'Think she did see the blighter, George?'

Gently merely looked blank. Against Miss Simpson there was certainly a question-mark. Her statement, which they had before them, added nothing to the account she had given. West she had left alone in the shrubbery and she had seen no one except the three girls. And yet . . . must not the assassin have been present at exactly that time, while West was still in the shrubbery? It had been dark, or nearly so, on the June evening, but still that question-mark had to stand.

'Only one bloke she would cover for.'

'She may have seen someone whom she took for him.'

'Oh come on, George!'

There is just a possibility. And then of course she would deny having seen anyone.'

Sir Tommy shook his head. 'Now you're trying to stand up for him! But it isn't going to wash, old fellow. Girl could have sworn it was a tramp, or Alec's burglar on the prowl. No, she knew whom she saw all right, that's what the emotion was all about. But we won't sit on her

52

too hard. Just a spot on those slacks is all we need.'

'And—if there isn't one?'

'You're being negative, old man.' But Sir Tommy's brow creased in a frown. 'I'm backing forensic. But if they don't come across, there's still a case for the fellow to answer.'

Gently let it ride. Without hard evidence, the case against Clarke remained indecisive and Clarke had shown no hesitation in providing the clothes he had been wearing. Could he be so sure that they told no story? He hadn't attempted any substitution. If he were guilty, it would have been difficult to manufacture such an appearance of confidence . . .

There was a tap on the door and Eyke entered.

'Here's his statement, sir—for what it's worth!'

Sir Tommy took it and glanced through it, then passed it across to Gently. It was brief and to the point: nothing was included that might offer a handle.

'How's the fellow taking it?'

'Hard to say, sir. Stubborn, I think is what you'd call him. I tried to get him to say a bit more, but this is all he would come across with.'

'Playing it clever, is he?'

'Close to his chest, sir. We're going to need all the goods we can get on him.'

Sir Tommy rapped the desk with his fingers. 'So where has that what's-his-name chappie got to?'

'Campsey, sir? He rang in just now. He's bringing one of the pub staff back with him.'

'So—he's on to something?'

'Seems so, sir. But he didn't go into details.'

In fact they had to wait another nail-biting twenty minutes before a car pulled in outside and, finally, DS Campsey ushered his prize into the office.

'Miss Collins, sir.'

A tall, blonde girl, she entered with a hesitant air. Around twenty-two or three, and dressed in a black frock that ended somewhere above her knees. She ventured a cautious smile.

'Sit down, my dear,' Sir Tommy said.

Miss Collins sat.

Campsey said: 'Miss Collins is the barmaid at the Brewer's Arms, sir. She says she knows Mr Clarke by sight and was serving at the bar yesterday evening.'

'Is that so,' Sir Tommy said.

'I thought you would like to talk to her yourself, sir.'

'Yes,' Sir Tommy said. 'Yes. Thank you, sergeant. You may go.' Campsey left. Sir Tommy eyed Miss Collins. 'Suppose we're sure of our facts, my dear?' he said. 'Know this Clarke fellow, do we—couldn't mistake someone else for him?'

'Oh no!' Miss Collins smiled. 'I met him when he held an exhibition and we've got a picture of his at home. He isn't a man one can easily forget.'

'Got a good look at him last night, did you?'

'Yes, it was me who served him at the bar. I told Jeff who it was we'd got there, but you know! Jeff doesn't care much about painting.'

'Couldn't confirm it then, this Jeff?'

'Well no, I suppose he can't. Though I did point Mr Clarke out to him. I expect he'll tell you, if you ask him.'

'Nobody else there who knew him?'

'I couldn't say. There may have been.'

Sir Tommy drew a deep breath. 'So carry on, my dear. Just tell us about what happened.'

Miss Collins looked puzzled. 'But—nothing did happen. He had a couple of pints, that's all.'

'You would know when he got there?'

She shook her head. 'Must have been getting on for nine, I'd say. The bar was noisy, so he went outside and only came back in for a refill.'

'What time was that?'

'I'm sorry. It could have been half an hour later.'

'And that's the last you saw of him?'

'Yes—I think. He wasn't in the garden when I went to collect the glasses.'

'He—wasn't.'

'No. It was after closing. There was no one in the garden then.'

'And what time would that have been?'

'Oh, around eleven. I expect he left by the

55

gate, most people do.'

Sir Tommy eased back a little in his chair. 'So the long and the short is this, my dear! As far as you can say, Clarke was there at nine-thirty, but he could have left at any time after that.'

'Well, he had to drink his pint before he left!'

'Needn't have taken him long, my dear.'

'It usually takes them at least half an hour ... and that was his second pint, too.'

Sir Tommy brushed it aside. 'Give or take. He could have been out of there by ten at the latest and that's what we needed to know. My dear, you've been a great help to us.'

Miss Collins looked a little alarmed. 'It's all right, isn't it?' she said. 'I haven't said anything—well, you know!'

'Just leave it with us,' Sir Tommy said. 'You've done your duty as a good citizen. Eykey, you take this lady's statement, then find a car to run her back to the Brewer's.'

Miss Collins rose uncertainly and allowed herself to be ushered out. Sir Tommy sat a moment brooding, then flashed a quick look at Gently.

'Well?'

Gently felt for his pipe. Then, slowly, shook his head.

'You mean to tell me—?'

'All we seem to have got is confirmation of Clarke's statement.'

'But—dash it all, George!'

56

'The lady can't tell us when *he* left the pub and her testimony suggests it was ten or later. Then he had a mile to walk to Beresford's, where he would have run into the people coming out.'

'But he *could* have left earlier!'

'We have no proof.'

'He could have dumped that pint and hooked it!'

Gently merely shrugged and went on filling his pipe.

'You, you're a devil,' Sir Tommy said. 'I believe you've been on Clarke's side from the start. But you can't deny this, he's still in the running. The lady's testimony doesn't rule him out.'

'Perhaps . . . not altogether.'

'You know it doesn't!'

'It just makes it a little less likely.'

'Ha!'

Sir Tommy stared meanly as Gently struck a match for his pipe. But at that moment the telephone rang and Sir Tommy snatched it up impatiently. He listened to it with a growing scowl, then slammed it down with a bang.

'Damn and damn!'

'Was that forensic?'

'The sods. They've done their preliminary check.'

'And?'

'Not a blasted sausage. And they expect their final report to be negative.'

57

Gently puffed. 'Perhaps Clarke is a lucky one . . .'

Sir Tommy drew a very deep breath.

* * *

'So now it is up to you, George.'

Much against the grain, Sir Tommy had been obliged to let Clarke depart, though not without an injunction to remain in town and to hold himself at their disposal. Then had followed a conference with Eyke and his second-in-command, Metfield, in which they had been directed to pursue enquiries at the Brewer's Arms and to interview every last participant at Beresford's soirée. A glimpse here, a sighting there, and the case against Clarke might still fall together . . . at least, it wouldn't fail for lack of trying! And, meanwhile, they were to keep an eye on the man himself.

'Any other instructions?'

Gently had shaken his head and shortly they were back again in Sir Tommy's Jag, driving through the gathering dusk, and silent till they reached the gate of Heatherings.

'I won't come in—got to get back, have to make a full report to Janet! And tomorrow there is a conference in Eastwich, so from now on it's in your hands. Quite sure you don't mind?'

Gently ghosted a shrug: his leisurely

58

weekend had long been forgotten.

'I'll have a word with Gilly,' Sir Tommy said. 'See if he can spare a few days after this is cleared up. OK with you?'

'OK.'

'Right, George. Then I'll get along. And don't forget to keep me informed—or there is someone at home who will never forgive me!'

The gun-metal blue Jag swept away and Gently turned towards the house. The Capels' car was missing from the sweep, but Reymerston's Renault still stood there. Reymerston was waiting at the door. He came forward impatiently, his eyes seeking Gently's.

'Well?'

Gently shook his head.

'But have they arrested Chris, you old devil?'

'No. Not yet.'

'Not yet! Then what you're saying is—?'

'Let's go in.'

Gabrielle was waiting in the lounge, with the same anxiety in her face; Gently went straight to the drinks-cabinet and poured himself a beer. He sat down and took a long pull. Then he sighed.

'It's like this . . .'

They heard him out in silence, Gabrielle with her eyes never straying from his. When he ended, there was a pause. Then she gave her head a little toss.

'So! It is this young man who paints that did it?'

'I am afraid Clarke remains the leading suspect.'

'Though he has no blood upon his clothes?'

'That would be possible, in such a mode of attack.'

'Ha. But is he not at the Brewer's when this attack is taking place?'

'Of that we have no certain testimony. He could have left in time to be present at the scene.'

'Oh God, I just can't believe it of him!' Reymerston exclaimed. 'I talked to him on the phone from Alec's. I could swear he knew nothing about it till he heard of it from me. He was shocked of course, who wouldn't be? But there was nothing furtive or guilty about him. I told him he had to expect a visit from you and it had him worried. But that was natural.'

'Did he tell you where he went when he left the soirée?'

'Yes. I asked him and he came straight out with it.'

'Did he say when he went from there?'

'Yes, after closing. And he came straight home.'

'No hesitation.'

'No . . . I don't think so. Oh God, you can't think of hanging it on him!'

Gently said: 'It all rests on that. At what time he left the Brewer's Arms. If he was there till closing we can probably exclude him, unless there are factors we don't know about yet.'

'What stupid factors?'

'Say, the attack occurred later.'

Reymerston stared. 'Oh, bloody hell! I can't see Ambrose hanging on there, waiting for him.'

Gently shrugged. Neither could he!

'It is so sad,' Gabrielle said. 'So sad. One of these young men dead and one to go to prison. And they are young people of talent, yes? The world, it was before them.'

'It's knocking poor old Alec,' Reymerston said. 'And he's been having it rough, lately. First his favourite nephew was in a car prang and then that son of his dropped out of college. And now this. I've got a feeling there won't be any more soirées for a while.'

Gently said: 'His son Lesley?'

'Fancies he's a poet too,' Reymerston said. 'And the nephew, he was trying to understudy his uncle. We reek with talent in these parts, George.'

It was after eleven when Reymerston left, with a final plea on behalf of Clarke. Before turning in, Gently strolled down the lawn to breathe in again the fragrance of the Walks. They lay in darkness, but a crescent moon had just emerged from cloud. Once again he leaned on the gate and let his thoughts find their own direction. A little over twenty-four hours since . . .

He smoked a pipe before returning to the house.

61

CHAPTER FOUR

He slept badly, and in the morning arrived at the police station later than he had intended. Something had been troubling him about the events of the previous day, a factor that he couldn't quite put his finger on. Several times he had awoken from a dream, a dream in which someone was trying to tell him something; but always the waking moment had failed to carry it into consciousness. Well, perhaps it would return to him later. As yet he was barely into the picture. Moodily, he drove back into town, the route taking him past the Brewer's Arms, outside which a patrol-car was parked. At the sight of it, he slowed; but then shrugged and drove on. Eyke met him in reception.

'We've taken statements from one or two of those people, sir. Johnson, the bloke who wrote the play, says he thinks he was next to leave after West.'

'Had he anything to tell us?'

'Only that he met young Beresford in the porch. Says he hung on to him to offer congratulations. When he got outside there was no one about.'

'He didn't see the girls.'

'They must have left by then, sir. Anyway, that's all he could tell us.'

Gently said: 'It doesn't quite square with young Beresford's statement that he went straight back into the house.'

'Perhaps he wanted to stop Johnson seeing what he'd seen, sir, and didn't feel the need to tell us about that.'

Gently shrugged. 'Perhaps! Was there anything else?'

Eyke shook his head. 'Only, now we've got the PM report. It's quite certain now when he died, because of what he ate just before he left. He'd had a sandwich and a cup of coffee, and they found them intact in his stomach. Like that they can nail the time down to between half-past ten and half-past eleven.'

So the picture was plain, if it hadn't been before: West had died minutes after entering the shrubbery. Perhaps while his hand was still to his cheek and Miss Simpson's running feet yet audible on the gravel. His killer had been present: West wouldn't have lingered there. That stake was already in a vengeful hand. There had been no words, no struggle, just the thud of blows, of a collapsing body. Was it credible that Miss Simpson had seen nothing, had not the smallest glimpse of the fateful presence?

'Any news from the Brewer's Arms?'

'Not yet, sir. I've got Metfield and Potton down there. We are trying to get a line on that man with a dog and the young couple that Clarke says were there. You never know.'

'And the man himself?'

Eyke hoisted a shoulder. 'We can't keep a watch on him all the time, sir! As far as we know he's sitting tight and we do know he took his bottle of milk in.'

From forensic there was a report on the stake that got them no further forward. Marks were available where a hand had grasped it, but the lichen had prevented an imposition of prints. Similarly the search of the shrubbery and the grounds had produced only negative results. A disturbance in the gravel of the former had been photographed, but nothing in the shape of a footprint occurred in it.

'Has anyone spoken to the parents?'

'Well—not since last night, sir! They were in a way, you can imagine. We had to take Mr West to the mortuary for an official identification.'

'He had no information for us.'

'Didn't like to ask him then, sir. I thought I might look in on him today. But I don't suppose there's much he can help with.'

Gently brooded. 'Where would I find him?'

Eyke shook his head. 'He should be at his business. But I doubt if he'll have gone there today, so he'll be at his house, which is in The Crescent. Shall I give him a ring?'

'Don't bother.'

'He's a decent bloke,' Eyke said. 'All this couldn't have happened to a nicer. And that young man was his only child.'

* * *

Market Street was where the estate agent had

his premises, a short thoroughfare of shops adjoining the High Street. Gently paused to stare in the window, at the range of coloured photographs of properties on offer. On the whole they seemed an up-market selection and included even one of the Georgian houses on the seafront. West's name on the fascia was painted a little off-centre ... had he been hoping to add to it: '& Son'?

The door opened on a short hall and a staircase, with entry to the shop on the left. Gently went in. Behind a desk, a short-haired blonde girl was scribbling on a form. She looked up quickly.

'I'm sorry, but today—'

'I wanted a word with Mr West.'

'I'm afraid he isn't in this morning. Though if you care to leave your name—'

Gently shook his head. The girl stared.

'Is it about—?'

'Yes.'

'Oh.' She fiddled with her pen. 'You'll find him at home,' she said. 'Though unless it's something very important . . .'

Gently shrugged. He looked around at the neat, well-furnished establishment, the filing cabinets, the tidy desk, the comfortable chairs for the accommodation of customers. Then at the girl. He said: 'Perhaps you would have known that poor young man?'

'Well!' The girl flushed-up. 'He didn't call here very often. He worked at the bookshop,

65

you know. He didn't have much interest in the business.'

'Would you have called him an attractive young man?'

'Yes—I don't know! Perhaps you would.'

'Did he ever make a pass at you?'

'Look—really! I don't have time to answer these questions.'

Gently nodded. 'But he was inclined that way. A romantic young man with an eye for the girls. Wouldn't you say that?'

She stared at him angrily. 'If you must know, yes he was! And yes, he did make passes at me and a fat lot of good it did him. I already have a young man and I'd got no use for Amorous Ambrose—that's what they called him! So, if you don't mind, I would like to get on with my job.'

Gently nodded again. 'Thank you for your time. But you understand these questions have to be asked.'

'Oh, I'm sorry.' She bit her lip. 'And I shouldn't have talked like that about Ambrose, not after what has happened. I'm sorry.' She threw him a look. 'You ... won't tell his father?'

'I won't tell him.'

'I wouldn't hurt him for anything. He's the best boss anyone could have.'

Gently left. He passed down the High Street, already busy though so early in the season, and took a turning that led to the common and the handsome houses that fringed it. The Crescent had a broad green before it. The West house was Number 6. It enjoyed a spacious prospect across the common, and down to the river and Walderness beyond. Gently hesitated before it: the curtains in the lower windows were drawn. Also, on the steps lay bunches of flowers, and black ribbon had been knotted in a bow to the door-knocker. A house of mourning . . . Feeling almost sacrilegious, he mounted the steps and rang the bell.

'Yes . . .?'

The door was opened by a tallish man in a black suit, behind whom, just visible down the hall, appeared the pallid face of a grey-haired woman.

'Mr West?'

The man merely stared at him.

'My name is Chief Superintendent Gently. May I come in?'

He heard the woman gasp and she vanished into a doorway.

'Is this visit necessary, Superintendent?'

'Regrettably, I need to speak to you.'

'But . . . at this time?'

'If I may.'

At last, silently, the man stood back to allow him to enter. He led him into a darkened lounge and quietly closed the door behind them. It was a large room with slightly old-fashioned furnishings which included a double-fronted bookcase. West would be in his fifties, a gaunt-featured man with dark hair combed very flat. He indicated a chair.

'You do understand? This has been a blow, especially to my wife. Ambrose was our only one. Even now, we can barely believe that it can have happened.'

Gently bowed his head. 'I met your son, Mr West.'

'You met Ambrose?'

'In the bookshop. He served my wife and myself. My wife thought him a very promising young man.'

'Promising . . . yes.'

'We were told of his book and she intended asking him to sign her a copy. It was then we heard the tragic news, only a few minutes later.'

West stared at the curtained windows. 'I won't conceal it from you, Superintendent,' he said. 'But I was never impressed by my son's ambition to make a name for himself as a poet. As a hobby perhaps, yes, an occupation for idle moments. But as the business of life—' He shook his head. 'For that, one needs a more serious purpose.'

'You would have preferred him to enter the firm.'

'I have to admit it. I own a very flourishing business. Had he wished, and if he had given his mind to it, there would have been a partnership waiting for him. But no.' West sighed deeply. 'Even in his teens the bug had bitten him. He dropped out of college to take

68

that job and has wasted his time ever since.'

'He dropped out of college?'

'Yes. And I blame the influence of Alec Beresford. Well, now his own son is going the same way, so perhaps he realises what he has done.' His eyes found Gently's. 'Are you going to tell me that what happened has no connection there—that it isn't all mixed up with those people and the goings-on at Beresford's?'

'The soirée perhaps offered opportunity...'

'Yes—the opportunity and the culprit! That's where you should be looking, for someone who imagined a grudge against Ambrose.'

'We are taking that into consideration.'

West looked away. 'You perhaps think I am raving. But some of those people aren't quite normal, they get these foolish ideas in their heads. I know, because I've had to live with it, with a young man who believed himself a genius. When that happens they stop being normal and then anything can happen. Do you understand?'

'I did meet your son—'

'Yes—when he was behaving himself in the bookshop! Living with him was another matter. Then you had to start asking yourself questions.' He was staring at the windows again. 'Let me take you up to his room,' he said. 'The room he spent so much time in. Perhaps that will give you a better impression.'

'His room . . .?'

'The one he called his study. But first, I'd better have a word with my wife.'

Abruptly he turned and left the room, and Gently heard a distant exchange of voices. In a little, West returned and beckoned Gently to follow him. They ascended first one staircase, then another, which ended in a bleak landing. A door opened off it. West threw it open.

'Behold . . . the workshop of a genius!' he said.

* * *

An unusual aromatic odour was the first thing one noticed in the attic of Number 6 The Crescent; an odour so potent that Gently could barely control a sneeze. At once one's eye was drawn to a poster at the far end of the room. It depicted the figure of a massive Buddha in the attitude of meditation. Below it a china Buddha figure presided over a miniature altar, with before it a blue bowl in which lay the charred remains of joss-sticks.

Irritably, West crossed to the window and flung it open.

'Don't think I hadn't spoken to him about this! But his mother always sided with him and nothing I could say would stop him.'

'Your son was a Buddhist?'

'So he said. At least, he never set foot in church.'

70

Other posters on the walls were of abstract paintings by anonymous artists and in a corner stood a statuette of equally abstract character. By the window a table served as a desk. A portable typewriter occupied one corner. Then there was *a* pad of multi-coloured sheets, an ink-pot and pen-tray, and a calendar. A bookcase near the table contained books on Eastern mysticism and on top of it lay half a dozen copies of the poet's first, and last, publication. It was entitled *Beyond Beyond*. Curiously, Gently picked one up; but the degree of abstraction presented by the verse called for more than casual inspection. He replaced the book.

'So—are you beginning to get the idea?'

'Do you mind if I smoke?' Gently said.

'Why not. It can't make the stink in here any worse.'

Gently filled and lit his pipe, his eye still wandering round that improbable room. On the floor, as in Clarke's bungalow, were a couple of variegated rag-mats. From the window the view was extensive, with just a glimpse of the sea down by the harbour. In fact, one could probably pick out the painter's residence among the distant straggle of roofs...

'Did your son invite his friends up here?'

West nodded. 'Some of Beresford's crew, no doubt! Young Darren was one of them, but I didn't mind him. He was working for me before his accident.'

71

'Darren . . .?'

'Darren Woodrow. He is a relative of Beresford's. The young fool took his mother's car one evening and ran it off the road. He's been off work since and I've had to engage a new assistant.'

'And he was friendly with your son?'

'He was one of them.'

'Can you remember some of the others?'

West frowned. 'I can't give you many names. There was Jason Adams, my manager's son, and young Luke Scott, who works for our solicitor. Jason is trying to be a writer, I'm told, and young Scott wants to paint. Darren had got the bug, too. But it didn't affect his work in the office.'

Gently blew smoke. 'Christopher Clarke—would that name ring bells?'

'You mean the painter?' West said. 'Yes, I've met him. He's different. He's a professional.'

'A friend of your son's?'

'I shouldn't think so. At least, he never brought him here. No—' West sighed. 'All Ambrose's pals were cranks and would-bes. A man like Clarke would have seen through them, this rubbish here wouldn't have taken him in.'

'He would have regarded your son as an impostor.'

West shook his head and stared at the view.

Gently puffed a few times. He said: 'I believe your son had a girl-friend.'

72

'A girl-friend!' West's head jerked. 'He's been having those ever since he could walk. Which one do you mean?'

Gently shrugged. 'Just the current one would do!'

'I'm sorry,' West said. 'I've lost count. His mother might know, but you can't talk to her. The last I remember was a Cathy Bennett, the daughter of the woman who keeps the cake shop. He took up with her in the spring, but I haven't heard tell of her lately.'

'One of the Beresford crowd?'

West nodded. 'Before that there was a Sarah. And last summer it was a Susan someone, he almost pined away for her. Wrote her poems she couldn't understand and swore they'd been lovers in a previous existence.'

'A passionate young man.'

'A young fool,' West said. 'But I shouldn't be talking about him like this.' He turned to face Gently. 'What can you think of me, carrying on in this way at such a time?'

Gently puffed. He said: 'Such young men can sometimes make enemies.'

'You mean . . .?' West's stare was searching.

'I mean we have to look at such a possibility.'

'Yes.' West's stare drifted. 'I can see your point, of course. But I don't see how I can help you. I can't recall any situations of that sort.'

'To your knowledge he received no threats.'

'None.'

'He never got into fights.'

73

West hesitated. 'Once, perhaps—now you ask. It happened a fortnight or so ago.'

'Go on.'

'Well, he came in late—I think he had been out drinking somewhere. And at breakfast the next morning I noticed he had a bruise on his forehead. I questioned him about it, but he didn't choose to be communicative. I got the impression that he was feeling ashamed of himself and didn't want me to press the matter.'

'He had been drinking?'

'That's certain. But the bruise could have been the result of a tumble. Luckily, my wife was on a visit to her parents at the time, so the matter was left there.'

'And this was the only occasion?'

'To my knowledge.'

'But . . . your son sometimes went drinking.'

West gestured impatiently. 'I suppose you can say that, though probably no more than any other young man. He had his own key, and came and went as he liked. We were often in bed when he came in. Once or twice, in the mornings, he looked the worse for wear and got a few shrewd looks from his mother.'

'Would you know who he was out with?'

'Not really. I would sometimes hear about it from Darren. Young Beresford and Luke Scott were part of the clique, but no doubt there were others of the same kidney.'

'The Beresford crowd.'

74

'Yes.' West stared savagely at the Buddha. 'And that's where you're going to find him, the one you're after. Some crack-brained animal with a grudge against Ambrose.' His eyes swept back to Gently's. 'Aren't you on to him yet—don't you have the smallest idea?'

Gently said: 'Can you suggest a name?'

'A name! No, I can't.'

Gently shrugged. 'Then all I can tell you is that every possible step is being taken and to ask you to bear with us with patience. And to accept our deepest commiseration.'

West was silent, his stare absent. By now the aromatic odour had faded. Sunlight from the window had reached the bookcase and was touching the little pile of books that lay on it.

* * *

Gently left without seeing Mrs West and directed his steps back towards the town; but, as he was passing one of the bungalows on the edge of the common, a door was thrown open and Elizabeth Simpson came running after him.

'Please—I must talk to you!'

'You have something fresh to tell me?'

'I've just been to see him—to see Chris. And there's a car outside there—you've got people watching him!'

Gently shook his head. 'Just checking that he is available. Was that all?'

75

'No—I've got to talk to you, I've got to make you understand.'

Tears were close. She was approaching the emotional state of the evening before. Aware of his reluctance, she reached out to clutch his arm.

'Look—we can sit out here on the bench—I promise you I won't make a scene. But I really must talk to you. I promised Chris that if I got the chance . . .'

'You promised Chris?'

'Yes. He said you were the only one I could trust.'

Gently sighed. 'Very well, then! If you really have something fresh to contribute.'

The bench was on the green with the prospect of the common before it. They had it to themselves, apart from distant strolling figures. Elizabeth Simpson threw herself down and clasped her hands on her lap. Gently sat. She remained silent for a moment, then turned an anguished face to his.

'Look—you believe Chris had a motive. But it isn't the way you think. Yes, he was jealous, there's no hiding that, but not the sort of jealousy that could lead to this. He isn't like that. We had talked it over. If I had been serious about Ambrose he'd have let me go. Oh, I know I was a fool over Ambrose, but I never meant it to go very far!'

'You had talked it over with Clarke?'

She nodded. 'He knew I had been seeing a

76

bit of Ambrose. I suppose it flattered me. He was very good-looking and everyone was sure he was going to be famous. He wrote me poems, sent me flowers, told me we were born to be together. I always treated it as a bit of a joke, but I have to admit I rather liked it. I went on walks with him on the common, and often had drinks with him and his friends. But nothing serious, I swear to you. It's Chris and I who really belong.'

'And—Clarke was jealous.'

She hung her head. 'He must have known I didn't really mean it. Chris and I have been together for ever, I used to know him when we were at school. But yes, he got moody, even though *I* tried to laugh it off. And then on Friday he made us have this talk and told me flatly that if I wanted it, he would let me go.' She dragged at her hands. 'I thought—I honestly thought I'd got it sorted! I told him that, from now on, I was going to give Ambrose the boot. It meant nothing to me, I said, it was just a game I'd been playing, and if it was really upsetting him then that was that—no more Ambrose. And that should have been the end of it, except that on Saturday Ambrose was in the clouds with his new book and I was forced to play along with him, though I did my best to keep it down.' She stared at her hands. 'And you know what happened next. That ghastly play. I couldn't get out of it. Paul had written the part with me in mind. There was nothing I could do, except play it flat, while Ambrose was acting his silly head off. And that did it. Chris cleared out. Oh, I could have thrown the script at Ambrose's head!'

The tears overflowed. She dashed at her eyes. A woman with a dog on a lead was passing. She gave Elizabeth Simpson an odd look and Gently a severe one; then tossed her head and marched on.

'Oh, I'm sorry!' Elizabeth Simpson said. 'I promised you I wouldn't make a scene. But thinking about that, I couldn't help it.'

'Clarke said nothing to you as he left.'

'No, how could he, in the middle of the play? But he gave me such a stare—oh, I was wondering if I'd lost him for ever! And then, again, I was angry too, because of the way he was showing me up to the others. But the play had to go on and somehow I managed to stagger through it. The rest you know. I tried to steer clear of Ambrose, but he ran after me as I was leaving.'

'I believe you passed someone in the porch.'

'Yes. Lesley. I simply brushed past him.' She broke off abruptly, eyes staring ahead. 'I suppose he didn't . . . you know?'

Gently nodded.

'Oh no!' Was there panic in that stare? 'He told you, did he?'

'He told me.'

'How Ambrose lugged me into the shrubbery?'

Gently nodded.

'Oh, blast him!' She went on staring at the distance. 'And he was there when the girls left—he saw me go bolting after them?'

'According to him, he went straight back in. He says he wasn't too happy with what he'd seen.'

'The little prig! So all he saw was me going with Ambrose into the shrubbery?'

'That's all he is admitting to.'

Her eyes jerked to his. 'You mean . . . ?'

'We have reason to believe he remained in the porch for some while after that.'

'For—?'

'At least until yourself and the girls were out of sight.'

'Damn him. Damn him!'

Her stare returned to the common, her hands gripped tight in her lap.

Gently said: 'Could it be just possible that Lesley was also jealous of Ambrose?'

'Him! You're not suggesting—'

'I'm told he is also a budding poet.'

'Yes, he is, but—'

'With perhaps . . . an eye?'

'Oh no!' She shook her head very decisively. 'All right, he may have made a pass, but I soon put the little creep in his place. Lesley Beresford knows full well that he has nothing to expect from me.'

'Yet—he did make a pass?'

'Forget it. He knows I wouldn't be seen dead

79

with him.'

Gently shrugged. 'Of course, I'm wondering what else he may have seen from the porch. And why he claims to have gone straight back in after seeing you and West enter the shrubbery.'

'But there was nothing to see!'

'Then why pretend he wasn't there?'

'Because—because. I don't know!'

'Could it be that he did see some third party, but doesn't want to be the one to give him away?'

'Oh hell—hell!' She hugged herself. 'And of course, if he did, it had to be Christopher. He's right, you aren't going to give him a chance. One way or another you're going to trap him.'

'I said, some third party.'

'And you meant Chris.'

Gently shook his head. 'As yet he is merely assisting our inquiry. If it was otherwise he would be in a cell.'

In anguish, she twisted herself on the bench. 'I could . . . tell you something. But you wouldn't believe me!'

'Something you . . . saw?'

'No! Nothing like that. Just something stupid that Ambrose said to me.'

Gently considered her. 'Well?'

'It was a few days ago, on the common. We were walking across by the links and he had the silly idea that someone was following us.'

'And was there?'

80

'No, of course not! You could see all around and there was no one. I told him not to be an ass and asked him who would want to be following us.'

'And?'

'He said someone had it in for him and that he needed to watch his step. He wouldn't tell me who or why, just that there was someone on his track. Well, I thought it was all pretence, that he was just trying to make himself seem interesting—men do that sort of thing! But perhaps it wasn't and there really was someone.'

Gently shook his head. 'How long ago was this?'

'Last week. The last time I went for a stroll with him.'

'And he would give no indication of who the person might have been?'

'No—I'm telling you. That's why I wouldn't believe him.'

Gently sighed. He said: 'You do realise that a certain individual would fit the picture and that if you persist in the truth of this anecdote you are doing that individual no favour.'

Her eyes widened. 'You can't mean—'

'I advise you to think about it.'

'But Ambrose would have said!'

'He may have thought it too obvious.'

'Oh my God!' She swung away from him.

Gently said: 'You were lying, weren't you?'

Elizabeth Simpson groaned. 'It's no use, is

81

it?' she said. 'Whatever I say, it's got to be Chris, nothing is ever going to change your mind.'

'So it was a lie?'

'No!' She sprang up. 'And I don't care how you take it! Chris is innocent. It wasn't him Ambrose meant. And if you won't believe that you must do the other thing.'

She hesitated a moment, torment in her face, then turned and ran towards the gate of the bungalow. Gently let her go. He sat a little longer, till he heard the slam of the bungalow door.

On the common, the lady with the dog stared across at him sternly; then turned her back.

CHAPTER FIVE

There were no longer patrol-cars on the sweep of the Beresford house, though tapes still guarded the approach to the shrubbery. Gently turned aside to enter it and paused to let his eye wander round the spot. The shrubbery was totally enclosed by its hedges. The only access was the rustic arch. A magnolia occupied the central bed, surrounded by begonias set to form a pattern. Than this, there was no other cover . . . was it possible for the killer to have lurked behind it unseen? Frowningly, Gently made a circuit of the bed, but the soil, the begonias, appeared undisturbed, while even in the twilight of a June evening the magnolia could have offered only an imperfect screen. He turned his attention to the yew hedges, inspecting them for any irregularity, but the result was the same. The shrubbery offered no hiding-place. The killer could not have waited there in concealment.

'So? Gently shrugged to himself; two alternatives remained. Either the attack had been made when the couple entered the shrubbery, or the killer had followed them in there; and, in either case, Elizabeth Simpson must have caught a sight of him. There remained only the faint possibility that he arrived after she had fled, but that required the improbability of West's having lingered in the shrubbery. And, if she had seen the man and denied it, could doubt remain of his identity?

He left the shrubbery and stood a while longer observing the surroundings of the sweep and the drive. Here, there was concealment in plenty in the laurels and shrubs that lined the latter, while on the side of the sweep opposite to the shrubbery, mature beeches guarded a grove of rhododendrons. Somewhere there . . .? The killer could have made his move as soon as Elizabeth Simpson left the shrubbery, but he would need to have been quick if he was to reach it before West emerged. Could she credibly have missed seeing him—or could any witness positioned in the porch . . .? Gently moved to the latter. From there, the whole theatre of the action was available, the departing girls, the fleeing Elizabeth, the figure advancing on the shrubbery: if such there had been at that moment. From the porch, one would see it all . . .

'You wanted me?'

Silently, behind Gently, the door had opened. Alec Beresford stood there, regarding him with cautious brown eyes.

'I saw you looking round—I've been doing the same thing myself! I don't think this place will ever be the same again. Is there news?'

Gently shook his head. 'Perhaps we can go over that evening again. Is your son in?'

'No, Lesley's out. But Melanie is here, if you need her.'

He ushered Gently down the hall and into the lounge with the art nouveau furnishings, and went to call his wife. Gently chose a chair that gave a view over gardens to the sea.

* * *

'It isn't too early for a drink?'

Still, there was that note of caution about Beresford. His wife, too, when she entered, seemed unable to make up her mind how to treat Gently. She gave him the briefest smile, then took a seat at a little distance. Today she was wearing a sober gown along with a handsome jade necklace.

'If you have a beer.'

'Of course, old man!'

He poured drinks adroitly at the bar in the corner, bitters for himself and Gently, and a gimlet for his wife.

'Cheers—if that is permissible!' He took the chair next to Gently. 'Now, if there is anything we can help you with to get to the bottom of this tragic business . . .'

Gently drank. He said: 'I have just come from a talk with Miss Simpson. She told me something about young West which I'm wondering whether to believe or not.'

'Liz told you something?'

Gently nodded. 'This happened less than a week ago. He appeared to believe he was under surveillance and that some person bore him a deep grudge. Apparently Miss Simpson didn't take him seriously, but she insists on the truth of her account.' Gently paused. 'I suppose neither of you can throw any light on the matter?'

They stared at each other. Melanie Beresford said: 'It wouldn't be like Liz to lie about it. On the other hand—well! Ambrose .. . you couldn't always believe what he told you.'

'A creative type,' Beresford said. 'You have to give them a bit of leeway. Ambrose could romance with the best of them when he had an audience and the mood was on him.'

'He would tell a tall story.'

'A complete fable, if he thought he could get

away with it.'

'And especially to the girls,' Melanie Beresford said. 'I suppose he thought they were the most gullible.'

She drank nervously, and Beresford drank.

'Yes, at the same time,' Gently said. 'Bearing in mind what happened only three days later. Can you recall nothing that might give it credence?'

Beresford took another quick sip. 'Has to be one person who stands out,' he said. 'But I don't have to name him. You've already got him in your sights.'

'Apart from Clarke.'

He shook his head. 'It could be anyone or no one. With a femme-hopper like Ambrose there are always miffed swains in the offing. I could name you one or two but I should only be wasting your time. A few insults may have flown, but I'm pretty certain it's never come to blows.'

Gently said: 'According to information, a fortnight ago he showed signs of having been in a fight.'

'A fight—?'

'He returned late from a night out, exhibiting a bruised forehead which he preferred not to explain.'

Another quick look between husband and wife.

'Do we know when this was?' Beresford said. 'I saw him pretty often in the bookshop and I

86

can't remember any bruise.'

'A fortnight or so ago is my information.'

Beresford eyed his glass. 'Well, I didn't notice it! But if he had been out boozing, then there's your answer. He must have been in some melée at a pub.'

'And of course he wouldn't want to advertise that,' Melanie Beresford said. 'Ambrose would have been much too proud.'

'Absolutely,' Beresford said. He took another sip.

Gently said; 'Still quoting information, I understand that West and his friends often visited pubs. No doubt you can name his companions to me, those who would currently be accompanying him.'

Beresford thought about it. 'If I must,' he said. 'But I'm pretty sure you'll be wasting your time. Honestly, we don't encourage any hell-rakers here. Our circle is purely a cultural concern.'

'Still?'

Beresford sipped. 'You could try Stephen,' he said. 'Stephen Burke. And young Jason Adams. They're both neophyte writers, always sending stuff off to magazines. Then there's Luke Scott, one of our brush-men and Paul Johnson, who wrote the play. And Peter Simms—I don't know! They could pick up others along the way.'

'And perhaps—your son?'

'Oh, Lesley!' Beresford twirled the glass in

87

his hand. 'I expect you will have heard about him, how he's trying to do another Ambrose.'

'He is our son, Alec!' Melanie Beresford exclaimed.

'I know, my dear, and I'll give him his due. But a modest degree at the UEA would have done no harm to his poetical prospects. Still, as you say, he is our son.'

Gently said: 'He was one of West's associates?'

'Yes and no,' Beresford said. 'He admired him and wants to go the same way, but he wouldn't have been human if he wasn't jealous.'

'He would have been one of his drinking companions?'

Beresford nodded. 'Him and his cousin Darren, before Darren's accident. But I can swear they never came in boozed, or with unexplainable bruises on their foreheads. So forget Lesley. And Darren is temporarily out of the running.'

'He took his mother's car,' Melanie Beresford said. 'They live together at the other end of town. That evening she was visiting us, and he pinched her car and had a pile-up. He wasn't badly injured, but he's still getting over it. Perhaps we shall see him at the next soirée.'

Beresford twisted his glass. 'He and Ambrose were close. We can only hope that what has happened won't prove a set-back. He was a fool to do what he did, but he has talent

88

and I have great faith in him.'

'Another poet?'

'No!' Beresford grimaced. 'One poet in the family is quite enough.'

'He's trying to write thrillers like Alec,' Melanie Beresford said. 'And Alec is quite certain he will be a success.'

Gently drank up. 'Perhaps', he said, 'you will provide me with a list of those people we spoke of. And then, if you don't mind, we will go over the events of Saturday again.'

'Yes of course,' Beresford said, and followed Gently in draining his glass.

* * *

'Another tot?'

Gently shook his head and contented himself with filling his pipe. Beresford, not to be beaten, brought out a capacious briar of his own. He filled it nervously and it took him a couple of matches to get it going. Melanie Beresford, meanwhile, had crossed to the bar to refresh her glass. Gently puffed slowly and let his eye stray over the handsome room.

'Was it in here that you held the soirée?'

Beresford nodded. 'We've always held them in here. At first there were only a dozen or so of us, but now we have to draft in extra chairs. People arrive here at seven and we fix them up with drinks. Then—it's a tradition—we give the painters the first session. We stand an easel at the end of the room and they take turns to exhibit their paintings, while your friend Andy stands by to comment and offer advice. It's a popular feature and gets us off to a good start. After that come the readings and recitations. Then it's the turn of our young theatricals, who usually put on a one-acter for us, and finally there's coffee, sandwiches and chat, and at ten-thirty we chuck them out. We've been running it for a couple of years now—Wolmering's Bohemia, Andy calls it.'

'And—on Saturday—you followed the same programme?'

Beresford fingered his beard. 'Well ... perhaps not quite! On Saturday we had something to celebrate, which rather influenced the proceedings. A young poet's first book marks an epoch, and we naturally gave him a bit of space—a signing session, some readings, a few words of congratulation from yours truly.'

'And then—the leading role in the play?'

'That was Derek's decision, not mine— Derek produces at our Little Theatre and he intends putting the play on there. But he didn't choose Ambrose merely as a compliment. He knew he'd give a good account of himself. And so he did. The part fitted him and he played it for all it was worth.'

'Which ... didn't please everyone.'

Beresford blew smoke. 'How am I going to put this?' he said. 'Chris was in a bad mood from the start, because of something Andy said

90

about one of his paintings. All right, Ambrose was poncing around Liz, but everyone could see she was trying to freeze him off. And the same with the play. It was almost comical, the way she put him down when he was trying to make a meal of it. Chris acted like an idiot. He must have realised it later. Ambrose never stood a chance of pulling it off with Liz.'

'Of course he didn't!' Melanie Beresford joined in. 'Ambrose was a laugh and she knew it. He had run after half her friends before her and none of them had lasted more than five minutes. It may have amused her to be his latest, but that's all. And she had clearly had enough.'

'Very clearly,' Beresford said. 'I can't imagine why Chris was such an ass. But, as I said, he was in a bad mood. So you probably have to blame it on your friend Andy.'

Gently puffed. 'So Clarke left and the play continued,' he said. 'Were there any other incidents, other expressions of discontent with the principal player?'

'I can think of none,' Beresford said. 'Setting aside Liz. The play worked well. Derek was satisfied. Judging from the applause, people enjoyed it.'

'When did it end?'

'Oh, tennish. Just in time for the coffee and sandwiches. Then there was the usual chatter and congratulations, after which the party began to break up.'

'Would you remember in what order they left?'

Beresford and his wife exchanged glances.

'I know Derek was the first to go,' Melanie Beresford said. 'He told me he had to let his dog out.'

'Some of the girls were among the first,' Beresford said. 'But I don't precisely remember who.'

Gently said: 'Perhaps your son would know.'

'Lesley?'

'He was in the porch to see them off.'

'Ye-es.' Beresford frowned. 'Yes, you might get something from Lesley.'

'We know he was there when West left and that he witnessed the incident with Miss Simpson. By his account he then returned here, but a witness places him in the porch a little later. Would you have known if he went out there again?'

Beresford shook his head. 'I was gassing with the others, not watching Lesley! But if that is what he says, you can probably take it as correct.'

'I . . . I think I saw him,' Melanie Beresford said. 'He did come back here, if I remember. It was soon after Ambrose left in such a hurry, after Liz.'

Gently considered her. 'You can be certain?'

'Yes. Certain!' But she avoided his eye.

Gently said: 'You appreciate the importance of this. Your son may have testimony that could

92

be vital. We know now that Miss Simpson left West in the shrubbery and that he was attacked very shortly afterwards. If your son had indeed remained in the porch he could have seen something that would offer us a lead.'

Melanie Beresford bent over her glass.

'I'm sure he would have told us,' Beresford said. 'The odds are he did what he said and only went back to the porch later. Now I think of it, I probably did see him. I seem to remember him pouring himself another coffee.'

'Yes—another coffee!' Melanie Beresford said. 'That's it, Alec. I saw him too.'

'Sorry,' Beresford said.

Gently puffed. He stared out of the window at the sea. He said: 'Perhaps you can remember who else was leaving at about that time.'

Another exchange of glances.

'Sarah went about then,' Melanie Beresford said. 'She came across to say goodbye to me. And I think she took Sue and Cathy with her.'

'Sarah Wright would that be?'

'Oh . . . you know about her, do you?'

Gently nodded.

'Well, that's all. Unless . . .?' She flickered a quick look at her husband.

Beresford fingered his beard. 'Paul,' he said. 'I think he left around then. That's Paul Johnson, our hopeful playwright. But perhaps you know about him too.'

'We have his statement.'

'Was he—any help?'

93

Gently merely watched the sea.

'Well, I don't know,' Beresford said, 'but those are the only ones we can think of. After Paul went the others hung on a bit, then they went off in a bunch. But by then, according to you, it would have been all over.' He breathed smoke. 'Dare I ask,' he said. 'Is there anyone in the picture besides Chris?'

'Alec!' Melanie Beresford exclaimed.

'I think we're entitled to know,' Beresford said.

After a pause, Gently said: 'Unless West wasn't pretending to Elizabeth Simpson, Clarke would appear to be the single prospect. As yet we know of no other with equal motive and opportunity.'

'As . . . yet?'

'The inquiry is proceeding.'

'But you have got some ideas?'

'Perhaps an open mind.'

Beresford stared at him frowningly and poked at his pipe. 'It could still have been an outsider,' he said. 'Not Chris. I won't have it. But a prowler is still a possibility. He could well have been lurking in the shrubbery, and then went berserk when he was spotted.'

Gently shook his head.

'But—why not?'

Gently said, 'The killer entered the shrubbery when West was already there. He had seen him enter and went there to find him. There can be little question of his intent.'

94

'He could have been lurking—'

'No. The shrubbery offers no concealment. The killer waited outside until West was left alone, then seized the opportunity that offered.'

'Oh, the devil!' Beresford frowned. 'But it still needn't have been Chris. Perhaps Ambrose really meant what he was saying to Liz.'

Gently shrugged. 'Perhaps.'

Beresford looked away, went on poking at the pipe.

'It could have been some maniac,' Melanie Beresford said. 'One of those with a thing about lovers. Wasn't there a case like that before, where the man used to creep up and shoot them? I've read about it somewhere.'

Gently watched the sea. He said, 'If you've no more to tell me we'll leave it there. Meanwhile I would be grateful for the list of those associates of West you mentioned.'

'Melanie—would you?'

Melanie Beresford put down her glass and rose. She went to the bureau, pulled out a pad and began industriously to scribble. The frown was still on Beresford's brow. He, too, looked out at the sea. Once or twice he seemed about to speak, but then, apparently, thought better of it. The list was completed, Gently folded it into his wallet and Beresford, silent, accompanied him to the door.

* * *

95

The door closed and once again Gently paused on the steps, surveyed again the prospect of the sweep, the descending drive, the taped entry to the shrubbery. And then he found himself observed. Lesley Beresford was hovering near the shrubbery. The young man was eyeing him nervously, seeming at any moment ready to dodge away. Gently stepped down and advanced towards him; defiantly, Lesley Beresford stood his ground. Slender, tallish, with lank, tangled hair, there was an air of vulnerability about him.

'It's—my turn now, is it?'

Gently found him a smile. 'Perhaps it is time we had another talk.'

'I don't know why, because I've nothing else to tell you!'

'Still, it may help to go over it again.'

'I—suppose I've got to.'

'Shall we go in there?' Gently indicated the shrubbery.

'You mean—?'

'Why not?'

'Well, if that's what you want!'

For an instant he hesitated, but then led the way round the tapes. Happily, the shrubbery had been tidied by Eyke's crew, the gravel rinsed and smoothed over. Lesley Beresford advanced cautiously, staying clear of the actual spot.

'Let's sit on a bench.'

They sat. Lesley Beresford kept his face

averted. Sun fell on the tangled hair, the slumped shoulders turned towards Gently.

Gently said; 'I paid a visit to the Wests. His father took me up to Ambrose's study. He told me that Ambrose often invited his friends there, on the evenings when he didn't meet them in town. I expect you will know the place.'

The shoulders moved.

'It still reeked of joss-sticks,' Gently said. 'It must have been intolerable in there when they were actually being burnt. Would you remember?'

'Yes . . . it stank!' The shoulders jerked impatiently. 'It was his thing. He always lit one. Temple Buddhism, my father called it.'

'Temple Buddhism . . .?'

'Not the real thing, just going through the motions. Mere superstition, my father says, the sort of thing the priests exploit.'

'So Ambrose's Buddhism wasn't genuine.'

'No. It was just a craze.'

'It stopped with the image and the joss-sticks.'

'It stopped . . .!' The shoulders hoisted.

Gently said: 'I ask, because Buddhism is the religion of non-violence. And at other times, away from his study, Ambrose appears not to have practised it.'

The shoulders froze. 'What other times?'

'Well—when you were out for a drink, for example. I'm told that quite recently he returned home bruised and the worse for wear.

97

Were you around when that happened?'

'When—?'

'Have you seen him in a fight lately?'

'What—do you mean?'

Gently said: 'Just that. Would you have been around when he collected the bruise?'

Lesley Beresford half turned, but kept his eyes fixed on the gravel. 'No,' he said. 'No, I wasn't. If he was in a fight it wasn't when I was with him.'

'But the bruise you might remember—a bruise on the forehead?'

He shook his head. 'I never saw any bruise!'

'No bruise . . .?'

'I keep telling you! If he did have a bruise it couldn't have been obvious.' He kicked at the gravel. 'We weren't like that. You seem to have got hold of the wrong idea. We did go out for a drink sometimes, but we didn't get drunk and pick fights. We'd argue, yes, but that's different, it was only about what we were doing.'

'And . . . girls, perhaps?'

'No! At least, it didn't often happen.'

'Just sometimes?'

He scuffed the gravel. 'All right. And you can make what you like of that.'

Gently nodded. 'On a different tack. We have been interviewing a number of people. Among them was Paul Johnson, who wrote the play you were reading on Saturday.'

Lesley Beresford stiffened. 'So what?'

'He remembers leaving shortly after West

and Miss Simpson. Apparently he met you in the porch, where you detained him with your congratulations.' Gently paused. 'You appeared to have forgotten the encounter in the account you gave yesterday.'

Lesley Beresford sat very still, with his eyes absorbing the gravel.

* * *

'That . . . was later!'

'Not according to Johnson.'

'Yes. I came out again, to see people off. I did go in, just the way I told you, but after a bit I went back to the porch.'

Gently shook his head.

'Yes!'

'Johnson had no reason to lie.'

'Then he's got it wrong, it had to be later. He's remembered it wrong, that's all!'

Gently said: 'West left in a hurry, attracting attention, and clearly Johnson must have noticed, since he says he left shortly afterwards and was in fact the next person to leave. He met you in the porch. This must have been straight after you saw West take Miss Simpson in here. You went out of your way to detain Johnson, and the question arises, why?'

'I—I don't admit this!'

Gently shrugged. 'Mustn't there have been something you didn't want him to see?'

'No! All that was later. And that's all I'm going to say.'

'How much . . . later?'

'It doesn't matter!'

Gently shrugged again. 'I think it does. For a while, you would be alone there, having seen what you had seen.'

Now Lesley Beresford did jerk round and his horrified eyes sought Gently's. 'You can't mean—!'

'I'm afraid I do. Because you were no great friend of West's, were you? A rival poet, his success bitter, and a little more than that. I had a conversation with Miss Simpson this morning and she advised me of the situation.'

'But you can't really!'

'There was opportunity. You were insisting on this yourself.'

'No!'

'You admit being mistaken?'

'I—!' He wrenched his gaze away and back to the gravel.

Gently said: 'Something you saw and something you didn't want Johnson to see. And it wasn't just the lovers coming in here, because they would have been out of sight by then. So . . . what was it?'

'It wasn't anything!'

'Then why detain Johnson?'

'I don't know! Perhaps . . .'

'Yes?'

'Perhaps . . . I don't know!'

Gently waited. Lesley Beresford sat staring, his face averted. The lank hair had fallen over his eyes; he swept it back with a sudden, desperate motion.

'Well . . .?'

'I may—I may have seen something!'

'Something?'

'Someone then, if you like! He was standing back here, near the corner of the house, as though he might have been watching people come out.'

'A man.'

'Yes, I'm saying!'

'A man you knew?'

'How could I have known him? He was standing in shadow, away from the windows. I only saw him as I turned back in.'

'After West and Miss Simpson had come in here.'

'After—after she ran off, if you must know! And I only noticed him because . . .'

'Go on.'

He heeled the gravel. 'He was heading in here.'

'You saw him go in?'

'No! Paul was just coming out and I thought—I don't know!'

'You wanted to stop Johnson seeing him.'

'Well—something!'

Gently said: 'I'm afraid you will have to do better than that.'

Lesley Beresford flicked at his hair. 'I thought—after what had been going on! I mean, we told you all about that. And as soon as I saw him . . . what else could I think?'

'In so many words, you saw Clarke out here?'

'No! I'm not going to swear it was him. It was too dark, I couldn't see him properly. It's just that immediately I was thinking . . .'

'But . . . someone not unlike him.'

'It—could have been anyone! Only, knowing what had happened . . .' He half turned towards Gently. 'I suppose I have to tell you! It wasn't just that. There was an earlier occasion when Chris saw Ambrose making up to Liz. I was having a drink with him. It was at the Horseshoes. We saw them go past towards the common. And he said something then about Ambrose regretting it if it went on for much longer.'

Gently gazed at him. 'And when do you say this was?'

'It's true, I'm not telling you a lie! A couple of weeks or so back, I can't remember exactly when.'

'And none of this you saw fit to mention till now?'

'I—no! I mean, I can't swear . . .'

'You were covering for Clarke?'

'I tell you I wasn't certain!'

Gently nodded. 'You just thought you would give him the benefit of the doubt.'

Lesley Beresford swung away from him again, kept his eyes on the gravel. He was breathing a little fast and the lock of hair had

102

fallen back across his face. Just then, footsteps approached from the direction of the house and Alec Beresford appeared at the tapes. He stared frowningly at his son, at Gently.

'I thought you had left, Superintendent.'

'Father!' Lesley Beresford jumped up.

'He's been putting you through it, has he, Lesley?'

'He—he thinks I saw Chris out here on Saturday. But I keep telling him—I can't be certain of that!'

'You saw—Chris?'

'That's what he thinks. I did see someone and I had to tell him. But it's true, I don't know who it was and I guessed what they would think if I spoke up.'

'I see,' Alec Beresford said. 'Well, you were a fool, Lesley, not to tell them straight out. It tends to look suspicious, old lad. The Superintendent was grilling us about you.'

'I'm sorry, Father.'

'Well—perhaps no harm done. You are quite sure you don't know who it was you saw?'

'Quite sure.' Lesley Beresford flicked his hair. 'He was just a shadow. I could only tell it was a man.'

Beresford nodded and turned his frown on Gently. 'Of course, you're only doing your duty, Superintendent,' he said. 'But I would sooner you had talked to Lesley in the house. To bring him in here was a shade melodramatic.'

Gently shrugged. 'It sometimes helps

103

memories. Your son's appears to have been a little selective.'

After a moment, Beresford echoed the shrug, turned his frown back to his son. 'What happens now,' he said. 'This is scarcely added grounds to bring a charge against Chris.'

Gently said: 'We will take your son's written statement and add it to those received. Eventually, it is to be hoped, they will lead us to the man we are after.'

'To . . . Chris.'

'Whoever it may be.'

The frown returned to him sharply. 'You mean—some other?'

'Whoever the facts fit.'

Beresford's stare lingered, then drifted away. 'Get along with him, Lesley,' he said. 'The sooner this is over the better. Put down just what you told him and don't let him wheedle out a fraction more.'

'But Father . . . I've told him everything now!'

'Then do your duty, like a good citizen. Too bad if he uses it against Chris, but that's not our affair.' He leered at Gently. 'Will he be back for lunch?'

Gently merely bowed his head.

'I'll tell Melanie,' Beresford said. 'Luckily it's only a salad today.'

He turned abruptly and strode back to the house; and Lesley Beresford followed Gently out of the shrubbery.

104

CHAPTER SIX

He obeyed his father; the statement related how he had gone to the porch to see people off, had seen West and Miss Simpson enter the shrubbery, the departure of the girls and the flight of Miss Simpson to catch them up. Then, as he had turned back towards the hall, he had glimpsed a figure advancing towards the shrubbery, a man, a man of average stature, but little more than a shadow against the bushes he emerged from. At once he jumped to a certain conclusion, though what he had seen gave no warrant for it, and in consequence had detained Mr Johnson, to help with assistance, if assistance was called for. Apparently, it had not been. No sound of a disturbance reached them from the shrubbery. When, subsequently, Mr Johnson departed, he was left with the impression that the shrubbery had been vacated during their conversation. He lingered a short while in the porch, but heard and saw nothing further, and so retired into the house and remained there till the proceedings concluded. Had he mentioned what he saw to anyone? No, he thought it better not to. He had heard no sounds at all proceeding from the shrubbery? No ... there had been a background of voices and laughter from the house. And— later on—had he not ventured out again and, perhaps from curiosity, taken a look in the shrubbery? No!—he denied this vociferously: why would he want to get mixed up with all that?

So he signed the statement and left, probably in time to take his seat for lunch, leaving Eyke looking after him with a wistful expression in his eyes.

'The young devil! He could have sewn it up for us. He was lying his head off, sir.'

'You think Clarke was the man he admits seeing?'

'I'm darned certain of it, listening to him. Clarke is one of theirs and they're going to cover for him, I'd say it was standing out a mile. And we wouldn't have heard a whisper of this if you hadn't put some pressure on him. Do you reckon he did tell his old man?'

Gently grimaced. 'I got the impression it may not have been news to him. But I could be wrong.'

Eyke shook his head. 'Not you, sir! They will have talked this over between them and what we've just heard is the tale they've come up with. He was in a spot, the young fellow, he was a bit too close to the action. They couldn't have him admit outright he'd seen Clarke, but there had to be someone out there besides him. So this is the tale, sir. He did see a bloke, but he couldn't tell who it was from Adam.'

'That could be the way of it.'

'It stands out, sir.'

'Young Beresford was holding something back.'

'But what else could it be?'

Gently found him a grin. 'If we knew that, we should probably know everything. But meanwhile'—he pushed the statement aside—'have we any news yet from the Brewer's Arms?'

'Ah, the Brewer's, sir! Yes, we've got on to the man with the dog. His name is Arnold, he's a regular there. Stringer knew who he was straight away.'

'Have you talked to him?'

'Campsey has. Says he took the dog out at about a quarter to ten. Remembers seeing a man sitting there on his own and a couple at a table across the other side.'

'Could he identify Clarke?'

'Just a man, he said. But it could hardly have been anyone else.'

'And—the couple?'

'We're not on to them yet, sir. Seems they weren't regulars at the Brewer's. But Jeff gave us the name of a few others who were there and we're checking to see if they can help us.'

Gently brooded a moment or two. 'Clarke would need to have left very promptly after Arnold saw him.'

'I don't know, sir. If he left at ten, he could have been at Beresford's by half-past.'

'It was cutting it close.'

Eyke looked down his nose. 'Can't see it matters so very much, sir. He only had to be there when they were turning out and he knew when that was going to be.'

'West's killer was already present in the grounds.'

'Give him five minutes,' Eyke said. 'If he left the Brewer's at ten he could have done it and we don't know he didn't leave before.'

Gently shook his head. 'It's a vital point and we need the testimony of that couple. Put extra men on it if you have to, but locating those two is a priority.'

'Right you are, sir.'

Gently gave him the picture of his encounters with West's father and Miss Simpson. On hearing the professions of the latter a gleam came into Eyke's eye.

'Clarke, sir. It has to be!'

'There is just a chance that West was spinning her a yarn.'

'I can't think why, sir. He knew who would be after him. I dare say he'd had a hint of it before.'

Gently shrugged, told what else he had learned from Lesley Beresford, and the gleam in Eyke's eye deepened. It kept adding up! The case against Clarke was slowly, inevitably, reaching a certainty. About the bruise he was less enthusiastic, unless it arose from an earlier conflict with Clarke. Gently provided him with the list of names of West's recent associates and instructions to query them on the matter.

'Mr West can probably give you the date when it happened, since it was when his wife was absent on a visit. Whether Clarke was involved or not, we need to know how he came by that bruise.'

Eyke promised he would do his best, but his expression said he felt urgency was not a requirement.

* * *

'A pint and a cheese sandwich.'

Business was slack in the bar of the Pelican. After being served, Gently carried his plate to the table by the window, where he had sat with Sir Tommy. Today, the dress shop across the street was open, with a stand of garments pushed out in the foyer. As he ate, his eye was caught by a figure in the window; but it was not that of Elizabeth Simpson. He ate and drank. Had she told him a tale? It was in her interest to start a red herring, to hint at some baleful presence pursuing the ill-fated young poet. Not Clarke, but another: a grimmer, more dangerous foe. One capable of the deed enacted in the shrubbery, of the intent to commit such a deed ... Was it credible? He chewed meditatively. Say, a wronged swain of paranoiac tendencies? A husband, even? One whose marriage had foundered as a result of the poet's activities? He shook his head. If such were the case, the affair would have gone the rounds, must have been suggested to his attention by one or other of those he had

109

spoken with. But if not this, then what? What mortal offence could West have given? He swallowed and took a pull. And yet, if Elizabeth Simpson had not invented it . . .?

Shrugging, he lit his pipe. It would need more support than he had come by yet. More credibly it was a device of West's to enhance his interest in the eyes of his would be beloved. He was a romantic, it bore the stamp. Her reluctance had perhaps been the reason for the invention. So, one would bear it in mind, but continue to pursue the main line of the inquiry . . .

He watched the woman in the dress shop put out some fresh garments, then drained his glass and got up from the table.

* * *

'I was in two minds about opening this morning. I got the news on local radio. I couldn't believe it, I rang their office. The girl there told me it was true.'

The bookseller's name was Henry Curzon and he was regarding Gently with incredulous eyes. A man in his fifties, going bald, with fleshy features and a moustache. He leaned on a counter piled with books, with shelves of them reaching to the ceiling behind him.

'I mean . . . Ambrose! He'd been here two years. He was a bit of a card, I know. But who on earth would want to do something like that

110

to him—and just when he was beginning to get somewhere? I tell you, I don't understand it. The fellow who did it must be bonkers.'

'West had worked here two years?'

'Yes, come August. And I don't mind telling you, he was an asset. The customers liked him, and he had a load of friends who used to come here and buy books.'

'Friends like himself.'

'Yes. Beresford's gang, if you know what I mean!'

Gently nodded.

'So there you are. And that book of his wasn't doing us any harm. I had arranged a signing session for him next Saturday and that would have brought a few people in. Honestly, I can't believe what's happened. Even now I look down there and expect to see him.'

'That was his department?'

'Yes, antiquarian. Or second-hand if you like it better!'

In fact the bookshop was divided in two by a pair of free-standing bookcases, with the far end devoted to second-hand stock and the exhibition of framed prints. It was furnished with a smaller counter and a chair. Followed by Curzon, Gently made his way to it.

'His friends visited him here?'

'Every day there would be someone. They would talk and argue the toss. He aimed to be a Buddhist, did you know that?'

Gently shrugged.

111

'Oh yes,' Curzon said. 'You can tell that from the title of his book. He had got as far as Zen. They used to argue it by the hour.'

'His friends would mostly be writers too.'

'Writers, painters,' Curzon said. 'All sorts.'

'People like young Beresford. And Christopher Clarke?'

'Don't know about Christopher,' Curzon said. 'He'll drop in for a book and a chat with me. But Lesley, yes, and Luke Scott and young Adams. And Stephen Burke and Pete Simms, and young Woodrow, he was a favourite. Darren.' He shook his head. 'You've heard what he did? You can't tell some of these youngsters.'

Gently said: 'Did his girl-friends never call here?'

'Ah,' Curzon said. 'I thought we'd get to that! I heard all about them of course, but on the whole he didn't encourage them to show up here. I can remember one tearful encounter, last year, but that's all. Ambrose kept them separate.'

'Who was the girl?'

'A Jane someone. Ambrose had ditched her at the last moment.'

'Anyone more recent?'

'No one who showed here.' Curzon hesitated, eyed Gently. 'Is that the angle?' he said. 'Trouble over a woman?'

'Would you know if it was?'

'Me! No. But I would have to agree it was a

112

possibility.'

'You can suggest no recent situation?'

Curzon thought, but shook his head. 'There was a bit of coolness between him and Lesley Beresford, only I think that was jealousy over his getting published. No wench involved there, at least to the best of my knowledge.'

'And of course, you wouldn't know if West had been in a fight lately?'

'In . . . a fight.' Curzon's eyes narrowed. 'You mean, in the last day or two?'

'Extend it to the last three weeks.'

Curzon slowly nodded. 'Yes . . . I think I'm with you.'

'So?'

'A fortnight last Friday. He turned up here looking a mess. He had been boozing, that was too obvious, and he'd got a bruise on his face— just here. What's up? I asked him, who did that to you? But I couldn't get much out of him, just that he'd been in a stupid brawl outside some pub, the evening before. I kept on at him, but he wouldn't let on what it was about, or who the bloke was.' Curzon paused. 'Do you reckon there's a connection—that it was the same sod both times?'

Gently shrugged. 'It's possible. Did he name the pub where this happened?'

'No, but you could try the Horseshoes, that's the one they usually go to.'

'A fortnight last Friday.'

'Yes.'

'Did any of his friends call in that day?'

Curzon hesitated. 'I'm trying to think! If I remember rightly, there were only two. Stephen Burke came in at lunch-time and later on young Simms.'

'Perhaps . . . Lesley Beresford?'

He shook his head.

'Christopher Clarke?'

'Yes—he did look in. But only to enquire about a book. He didn't have anything to say to Ambrose.'

'Is there anything else you can remember?'

'That's about it,' Curzon said. 'I made him swab the bruise with TCP and that helped to make it more respectable. But—' He frowned. 'Could there really be a connection? I mean, there's a bit of difference between a pub brawl and what happened at Beresford's! It wasn't the booze talking there, more like a maniac on the loose.'

Gently stared at the counter, the chair. 'We have to look into such things,' he said.

'I know—but still!' Curzon also stared at them. On the counter lay a notepad with scribbles on it. 'I suppose—' he began, but just then the doorbell rang and a customer entered. Gently picked up the pad. The scribble was incoherent. But two words of it were decipherable: they were 'Liz' and 'tonight'.

*　*　*

He took the long way round to Harbour Road,

114

by the cliff path and the green, a route overlooked by the windows of the Beresford house and with a prospect of the bay. Misty ships trod the horizon, one a ferry-boat heading for Holland. He paused a moment to take it in, to breathe the gentle breeze from the sea.

This afternoon no patrol-car was parked near the timber bungalow—doubtless Eyke had found other tasks for his limited establishment. The rear of the Lada peered from its garage, but the half-door was closed and Gently heard no movement within when he applied himself to the knocker. Had the painter seized on the opportunity . . .? A narrow path was squeezed between the dwelling and its garage. Gently followed it to a painted door that opened with a noisy squeak. The scrubby lawn lay behind it: and stretched on a sun-bed, Christopher Clarke. He didn't get up, merely stared, then jerked his gaze towards the common.

'Is this it, then? I'm packed and ready!'

Gently advanced to the sun-bed. Clarke wouldn't look. He kept his eyes turned to the common, across the low hedge and the dyke. Gently sighed and took out his pipe.

'Were you thinking of making a confession?' he asked.

'No, I'm bloody not! And if that's the idea you can clear off again.'

'So then . . . a little talk?'

'I've nothing to say to you.'

'Perhaps a few things that I ought to know?'

'I've told you everything. And if you've come to arrest me, just get on with it, that's all.'

'You don't feel co-operative.'

'Just get on with it! Do you think I haven't been expecting this?'

Gently lit his pipe. There was a crude bench beneath a tree already laden with small apples. He brushed aside a couple of windfalls and seated himself on the bench. Clarke pulled round to observe him, then returned to his scrutiny of the common.

'I believe you have seen Elizabeth,' Gently said.

A chuck of the head was Clarke's only response.

Gently said: 'You will be glad to hear that she sticks by her statement of what happened on Saturday.'

'So . . . bloody what.'

'She says she saw no one. After she left West in the shrubbery. Unfortunately'—Gently puffed—'that doesn't quite square with the testimony of another witness.'

'It—!'

'A man was seen there. He was seen to enter the shrubbery. This immediately followed Miss Simpson's departure, so it is not impossible that she would catch a glimpse of him.'

Now Clarke did twist round. He swung his legs to the ground so that he could face Gently.

116

There was alarm in the hazel eyes and dismay in the drooped mouth.

'Who—told you that?'

'Does it matter who?'

'I want to know the bastard's name! He's saying it was me, is he—is that the idea—he's trying to put me on the spot?'

'He reports what he saw.'

'Oh, bloody hell! But if he says it was me then he's a liar. He must be some swine who's got it in for me, who'd stop at nothing to land me in it. What's his name?'

'I can't tell you that.'

'No—and you wouldn't if you could.'

'He was situated where he could have been an observer.'

'And you're going to believe every word he says!'

Gently puffed and lent his gaze to the common. From the garden one had a comprehensive view: the grassy sweep sloping down from the town to the marshy levels, the river and the harbour. Here and there strollers, in the distance a pavilion, and, over all, the remote presence of a water-tower. The low hedge presented little obstacle. A gap occurred in it, with a plank across the dyke.

Gently blew rings. He said: 'Miss Simpson speaks of walks she took on the common.'

'I don't want to hear!'

'She relates a conversation she had with West.'

117

'Must I bloody listen?'

'He was under the impression that someone had them under surveillance. That, of course, would be possible from here. He went on to say that he felt himself threatened and that he knew who the person was.'

Clarke's fists clenched. 'And it has to be me?'

'He mentioned no name to Miss Simpson. She could see no sign of anybody observing them and was inclined to think that West was romancing.'

'But of course—it was me!'

Gently shrugged. 'He may have caught sight of you out here.'

'Yes—with a pair of glasses, no doubt, and a cudgel waiting to bash him with!' Clarke glared at Gently's pipe. 'Don't you think I have better things to do—better than watching a creep like West poncing about on the common?'

Gently said nothing.

'Well I have,' Clarke said. 'And you can bloody believe it or not. So if the louse felt himself being threatened it was by his conscience. Not by me.'

'He had no occasion to suppose it,' Gently said.

'No. He sodding hadn't.'

'You issued no verbal threats.'

'No.'

'To him—or another?'

'Bloody . . . no!' He stared past Gently at the apple tree, his mouth bitter, his eyes desperate.

118

He said; 'Look—can't you try to believe me? Andy told me I could trust you! And whatever any bastard says, I never went back again to Beresford's. I'd seen enough, I cleared out. Liz must have told you we'd talked it over. If that's what she wanted, OK, but I couldn't bear watching it going on. Can't you understand that?'

Gently paused before nodding.

'I wanted out,' Clarke said. 'I was wrong, I know that now, but all I wanted then was to get away. I'd lost Liz, or so I thought. I wanted space, distance. And I wound up at the Brewer's Arms and bloody stayed there till turning out.'

Gently said: 'We've talked to the man who brought out the dog.'

Alarm was suddenly in Clarke's eyes. 'He told you, didn't he? He saw me there?'

'He saw you,' Gently said.

'Thank God for that!'

'At a quarter to ten, by his reckoning.'

'So?'

Gently said: 'We can't put you there any later than that.'

'But—!'

'The distance is about a mile. You could have walked it in fifteen minutes. The critical time is around a quarter to eleven. You could well have been back at the Beresford house.'

'But . . . I was still at the Brewer's Arms, then!'

119

'We have no evidence of that being the case.'

'Yes, that couple . . .!'—He broke off abruptly.

'We have been unable to identify them.'

He jerked away, stayed staring at the ground, his fists clenched very tight. 'Then I'm for it—nothing else counts?'

'Not unless you can prove you couldn't have been at the spot.'

'Oh, God Almighty!'

He was silent some moments, eyes still fixed, fists working. Gently drew on a pipe that was cold. At last, Clarke pulled himself round again to face him.

'Look . . . it doesn't have to mean anything at all! I mean, the time when I left the pub. I could have gone anywhere at all, it didn't have to be back to Beresford's.'

Gently shrugged.

'And then there's my clothes. You didn't find anything on them, did you? And . . . well, there must have been blood around, or you wouldn't have bothered with them.'

Gently shrugged again.

'They've got to give me a chance—it's all on what happened back at Beresford's! So they think I stand out a mile and they may be right. But it doesn't make me guilty.'

Gently knocked out his pipe. 'Last Thursday fortnight.'

'What . . .?'

'Can you give me your movements on that

120

evening?'

'My . . . movements?'

Gently nodded. 'Where you went. Who you were with.'

'But what has that got to do with it?'

'You don't wish to tell me?'

'I—I don't bloody remember, do I? I may have been working, I often am. Or I could have gone out for a pint.'

'A pint—where?'

'I don't know!'

'Would it have been, say, at the Horseshoes?'

'At the—?' There was caution in Clarke's eyes now. 'Look, do you mind telling me what this is all about?'

'You don't know?'

'No, I bloody don't!'

'Didn't you see West and your friend pass by that evening?'

'I—'

'And didn't you make some remark on it to your companion?'

Clarke's eyes clung to his, the mouth gaping below.

Gently let his gaze stray to the common. He said: 'Later that evening West was in a fight. He appeared the next morning bruised and out of sorts. He was unwilling to explain his condition, other than that he had been in a foolish brawl. Quite clearly he had been badly beaten-up and was ashamed to admit what had been the cause

121

of it. His condition has been independently testified to by his father and by his employer.' Gently paused. 'I have to ask you again: what were your movements on the evening in question?'

For a long moment Clarke stared at him, then wrenched his eyes away with a despairing groan.

'Well?'

'What's the bloody use! You're going to have me for this, aren't you?'

'Were you in the Horseshoes that evening?'

'What do you care?'

'And did you make the threat which has been reported to us?'

He pounded his thighs. 'It's a bloody lie! But it suits your sodding book, doesn't it?'

'You made no such threat.'

'No. Never!'

'And there was no later encounter between yourself and West?'

'What's the use of me denying it?'

'Was there, Clarke?'

He hammered his thighs.

Gently said; 'I regret the facts seem to suggest it. That, angered by the sight of West in the company of your friend, you sought an opportunity to have it out with him. This led to the physical encounter that left him in the state he was seen in the next day. Does that seem unreasonable?'

'I'll get my bloody things!'

'Then . . . you admit that you were responsible?'

He hurled himself up from the sun-bed and stood glaring at Gently, his fists working.

'I didn't do it! I didn't beat him up and I didn't kill him! You can think what you like, do what you bloody like, but I'm not the rotten sod you're after. Yes, I was sick about him and Liz, but I never lifted a finger against him. You can believe what you frigging like, but you're looking at an innocent man.'

'Whoa, hold it!' Gently said. 'We have to put these things to you.'

'Oh yes—and I'm for it, aren't I? It's all adding up just the way you want it!'

'Your denial will be noted.'

'Sod my denial!'

'Our inquiry is still in progress.'

'And what good will that do me?'

'It could lead', Gently said, 'to establishing the innocence you are claiming.'

'Bloody ha!' He pulled away, stood staring out over the common. 'Then—you're not going to take me in. I've got to wait till you can put the last nail in my coffin?'

Gently also rose. He knocked out his pipe finally against the apple tree. He said: 'It still rests largely on this: the time you set out from the Brewer's Arms.'

'It—rests on that!'

Gently nodded.

'But . . . if some rotten sod should lie about

123

it?'

'We would naturally check any testimony that we received.'

'But—!'

Gently also stared at the common. He said: 'Is there anything you would like to add?'

Clarke simply kept his eyes ahead. But the knuckles of his fists were white.

'So we'll leave it for now,' Gently said. 'I'll just remind you that your presence is required here. And perhaps that the inquiry isn't over yet and that we won't be jumping to any conclusions.'

Clarke's mouth was bitter. 'But I'm still Number One!'

'Regretfully, you have to expect it.'

'Yes . . .!' His eyes never left the common.

Gently sighed and pocketed his pipe.

He felt like a drink and sought one at a pub on the corner of the green. There, he was surprised to find Lesley Beresford nursing a glass at an outside table. Seeing him, the young man started up and almost took to his heels across the green. Shaking his head, Gently watched him go: he had left a half-full glass behind him.

Lesley Beresford, who had seen . . . someone.

And who had testified to that threat in the Horseshoes . . .

Over his drink, Gently watched the sea, but barely noticed the ships that traversed the horizon. Then his eye returned to the abandoned glass, and he shrugged and drank up.

Across the green, in the gateway of his father's house, Lesley Beresford had lingered, watching him.

CHAPTER SEVEN

'Your name is Jason Adams, of 16 Calthrop Road?'

He was the fourth on the list of Ambrose West's associates. Before him Stephen Burke, Peter Simms and Luke Scott had provided statements, varying little in detail. Yes, they frequently spent evenings together, more often than not with Ambrose of the party, and yes, if they didn't begin there, they often wound up at the Horseshoes. They would stroll on the beach or the common, discussing and comparing their endeavours. Luke Scott brought his sketch-pad and would sometimes amuse them by dashing off lightning caricatures. But West was clearly their star player. With them, his success had never been in question. The acceptance of his book had been long anticipated and was the occasion of boisterous celebration at the Horseshoes. But their memories were hazy of the critical Thursday: none could precisely remember that evening. And disturbances . . . fights? They indignantly denied them! Such was not the way of the Wolmering Bohemians.

'You were a friend of West's, Adams? You were often in his company?'

'Yes ... I suppose! But I don't know anything about what happened Saturday night.'

'You would spend evenings with him.'

'Yes, we all did—'

'Have drinks with him—that sort of thing?'

'It wasn't just that!'

'But you were often at the pub.'

'Yes, I suppose. If you want to put it that way.'

He was a stripling of about twenty with nervous, anxious eyes, dressed in jeans, trainers and a multicoloured jacket. Eyke regarded him almost paternally as he sat uneasily before the desk. The son of West senior's manager, he worked at an ironmonger's in the High Street.

'Tell us something about those evenings, Adams. I dare say, now and then, you had a drop too much.'

'No—well, not often! Mostly, I just stuck to a pint.'

'What about West?'

'Well ... sometimes. But Ambrose liked a scotch as well.'

'Got noisy, did he?'

'I wouldn't say that.'

'A bit touchy?'

Adams shook his head, glanced uneasily to where Gently sat nursing his pipe. 'It—it didn't often happen, that sort of thing. Only if one of us had something to celebrate. Like when I got a poem in a magazine ... I suppose, then, I may have taken too much. But it wasn't usual. Mostly, we only went to the pub later. If it didn't rain we would go for a stroll and sometimes Ambrose invited us back to his room. I ... well, I wasn't keen on that! He used to burn joss-sticks and it got on my chest.'

Eyke leered at Gently. 'And his girl-friends,' he said. 'Didn't he sometimes bring them along?'

'You mean—?' Adams pulled himself up short. He blushed. 'No—not when he was with us.'

'You never saw them?'

'No!'

'But you'd know about them, of course.'

Adam's blush deepened. 'Yes—well! We all knew about them, didn't we? He had a name for it, Amorous Ambrose. And he didn't mind talking about them.'

'About the latest.'

Adams said nothing.

'Come on!' Eyke said. 'You know who she was.'

'I—I don't want to talk about that.'

'Liz Simpson,' Eyke said. 'And I'm asking you.'

Adams stared down at his hands.

Eyke sighed. 'Ah well ... it doesn't matter! We've got all we need about that. Let's get on to something else. Last Thursday week—can

127

you remember that?'

'Last Thursday week—?'

'That's what I said. Was it the Horseshoes you were at that night?'

Adams looked startled. 'Yes . . . I think. But I don't remember anything happening there.'

'You don't remember the booze-up?'

'No, I don't. Not if it's the evening I'm thinking of. That was the day I got the cheque for my poem and only a few of us turned up.'

Eyke stared at him. 'But there was some drinking.'

'Yes . . . but not what you'd call a booze-up.'

'Young West got pissed, for one.'

'Ambrose? But Ambrose wasn't there.'

Eyke's stare hardened. 'Wasn't . . . there?'

'No. There was only Stephen, Pete and myself. I wanted to tell Ambrose about my cheque, but that evening he didn't turn up.'

Eyke gazed at him. 'You're sure you've got it right—this was last Thursday week?'

'Yes, I told you. I'd got my cheque. I paid it in the same day.'

Eyke kept staring. He shook his head.

Gently blew a ring. He said. 'I expect you saw your friend later and you were able to tell him about the cheque then.'

'Yes, I saw him on the Saturday, when I called in at the bookshop.'

Gently said: 'Did you notice something about him?'

'Something . . .?'

128

'Something about his face.'

'Oh—that!' Adams half shrugged. 'He said he'd bumped his head against a door.'

'Against—a door?'

'That's what he told me. That he'd tripped and bumped his head.'

'No mention of a fight.'

'A fight?' Now it was Adam's turn to stare.

Gently puffed. 'One other thing. Wasn't Lesley Beresford with you that evening?'

'Lesley? No, he didn't show up. We hadn't been seeing so much of him lately. He was miffed over Ambrose getting his book accepted, when he was only getting rejection slips.'

'There was jealousy between them?'

'Well—Lesley! He's always been one to take offence. He can't help remembering whose son he is and he thinks it should give him an edge.'

'And that evening you saw nothing of him.'

'I believe he had something going on at home.'

'And none of the others ... say, Chris Clarke?'

He shook his head. Then his eyes jumped to Gently's.

'Thank you for your time,' Gently said. 'Now all we require from you is a written statement. We would like you to describe that Thursday evening and also to mention what West told you about his bruise.'

'But—!'

Eyke nodded to Campsey, who was standing by.

'This way,' Campsey said.

Still staring at Gently, Adams got to his feet. And followed Campsey.

*　*　*

'A pity about that, sir.' Eyke had lit a cheroot and sat exhaling meditative smoke. 'We nearly had Clarke tied in there. He could still have been in the pub earlier and said what he did to young Beresford.'

Gently shrugged: it was barely possible, but Adams's account seemed to rule it out. Almost certainly it had been another evening when the painter had uttered that threat. On the Thursday the script had read differently. West was absent from the usual gathering, again pursuing—the odds were high—his amorous course with Miss Simpson. And if Clarke had observed them, it was not through the window of the Horseshoes, but more likely from the lawn of his bungalow as they dallied on the convenient common. And then . . .? West had clearly been drinking, most likely after parting with Miss Simpson; Clarke could have been waiting outside the pub and then have followed the poet to some deserted spot. Yes, it all added up. And yet . . .? Still, West had continued to pursue Miss Simpson!

'He lied about his injury to Adams.'

'He lied about it to everyone, sir. He wasn't going to admit he'd had a beating from Clarke, he would never have been able to live it down.'

'Nor does it seem to have taught him a lesson.'

'Well there you are, sir! You're only young once.'

'His attentions to Miss Simpson remained quite open.'

Eyke shook his head and tapped ash from his cheroot.

Gently said: 'Just in passing! Does young Beresford have any sort of a record?'

'Young Beresford . . . ?'

'He doesn't appear to have been the best of friends with West.'

'Well . . . I don't know, sir! But since you're asking, we did once have occasion to give him a caution. For threatening behaviour it was, he got a bit obstreperous at a pub one night. But you can't be thinking . . . ?'

Gently said: 'It wasn't only vocational jealousy between them. According to Miss Simpson young Beresford also tried his luck with her.'

'Young Beresford did that?'

Gently nodded. 'And on that Thursday he wasn't with his friends.'

'But . . . all the same, sir!'

'And we have to remember it is on his testimony that Clarke uttered a threat.'

Eyke stared at the cheroot. 'I suppose we

131

have to look at everything, sir. And if it wasn't Clarke who beat West up, then you could make a case against young Beresford. Only . . . I don't know!'

Gently said: 'According to his statement he caught sight of a figure entering the shrubbery on Saturday night, a figure he would like us to think was Clarke, but whom he takes care not to swear to. We have only his word for this. For a short period he was in the porch alone. He is next seen by Mr Johnson, whom he overwhelms with nervous congratulations. What we don't know is how long he was alone there between the flight of Miss Simpson and the encounter with Johnson.'

Eyke drew quick puffs. 'When you put it like that, sir!'

'He had motive and perhaps opportunity.'

'He could have been in and out of there and got almost caught by Johnson.'

'He could also have been West's assailant on the Thursday.'

'Yes, sir—I see what you mean. And then, seeing what he saw on Saturday, a rush of blood and that was that.' Eyke puffed very hard. 'You've got a point, sir. It could *be* the answer to a lot of things. Only . . . well, you can't overlook Clarke. If young Beresford has a case, Clarke has a better one.'

Slowly, Gently nodded. 'But young Beresford hasn't told us everything,' he said. 'He saw more than he's admitting to, standing alone there in the porch.'

'You think he could swear to Clarke, sir?'

'Perhaps.'

'It would wrap it up in a flash, sir.'

Gently managed a smile. 'Until then, we need that couple from the Brewer's Arms. Any word of them yet?'

'Not yet, sir, but we're on to a man who might know them. He was seen talking to them that night, but he's a rep and he's away all day.'

'Have a man lying in wait for him,' Gently said.

'Don't you worry, sir,' Eyke said.

* * *

He rang Gabrielle from Eyke's office before strolling back to the green. No Lesley Beresford was lingering there now at a table at the pub on the corner. Gently crossed to the gates of the house and remained a moment peering up the drive, from which he could just glimpse a corner of the house and a shred of the tape that still guarded the shrubbery. Nothing stirred there. He turned away and checked the time by his watch: then set off at a brisker pace back across the green and into the town.

The location of the Brewer's Arms he knew and the walk took him precisely fifteen minutes, first threading the High Street, then the brief suburbs and finally crossing the low

133

bridge that marked the town's limits. The pub, a tall, white-plastered building, occupied a site at a junction, with a tree-shaded garden accessible from the road by a gate. Fifteen minutes . . .! The pub was open. He entered its spacious bar. At this time of day there were few customers and only the landlord was at the counter.

'Just a half!'

The man gave him a stare, as though he found the face familiar, but nothing was said and Gently carried his glass through an open door into the garden. He glanced round it and selected a table . . . could it have been the same that Clarke had sat at? The garden consisted very largely of a lawn, with the bench-type tables occupying the perimeters. It had no lighting, other than a lamp over the door through which he had come, and the overhanging trees would have added gloom to the twilight of a June evening. If Clarke had sat there, the courting couple would probably have chosen a table on the other side; near the gate. Was it possible for them to have been unaware of his departure?

Gently took his seat, drank, automatically felt for his pipe. In his mind was still the picture of the lawn of the bungalow, with the despairing figure of the painter stretched on the sun-bed. A picture of guilt? He found himself frowning. The facts all declared it, and yet . . . He shook his head, struck a light, sent a

134

puff of smoke towards the boughs overhead. Something about him, about Clarke, was keeping the door just a little ajar . . .

He was no fool and he was no failure. At thirty, he was established in his vocation. By hard work and determination he had made his way to where he was now. He owned his bungalow, his car, was secure in a market for his wares and no doubt was preparing, before this had occurred, to invite the woman of his choice to join him. A picture of a determined character, of one who knew where he was going. Was it credible that he had been thrown so far off-balance by the antics of a ricochet lover like West?

West's proclivities were well-known: they had earned him a contemptuous nickname. A few weeks, at the most a few months, were the extent of his hectic affairs. Each new attachment was the love of his life, he worshipped her, courted her with amative verses, swore they had been lovers in a previous existence: and after that, dropped her flat. He was a joke: Clarke must have been aware of it. Certainly, Elizabeth Simpson was. Unwisely, she had been amused by it, but she had never been taken in, and after the *éclaircissement* with Clarke, was prepared to end the connection. Must Clarke not have seen that, in spite of Saturday's events? Could the play-acting have deceived him so completely? He was no fool! Disgust may have removed him, but surely not

135

a jealous rage such as would lead to what happened. In effect, even such an encounter as appeared to have happened earlier didn't fit in with the character of the man . . .

So?—Gently took a long pull. Another picture was taking shape in his mind. A picture of thwarted ambition and desire, of a solitary figure on the steps of a porch. One who had seen the object of that desire accosted by the object of his hate, had watched her drawn into a cover of opportunity, from which moments later she had taken flight. A better picture? Given the construction most favourable, Lesley Beresford still left the impression of having something to hide, of knowledge he was unwilling to impart, or of testimony other than the truth. And what other could that be, if not a confession of his guilt? Motive and opportunity had been his: Paul Johnson might have caught him still trembling from the deed. A better picture . . .? Gently drank again. Once more, it left something to be desired. So Lesley Beresford had information he wished to hide, but could one safely push it further than that?

But then, if neither picture fitted, they seemed left only with Beresford senior's surprised intruder, or the bookseller's maniac on the loose, unless . . .? Gently shook his head. Their leads, alas, ended there. One could but continue to pursue them, in the absence of fresh pointers coming to hand.

He drank up and only then was aware of the

presence of another in the garden. A man dressed in a suit had emerged from the bar and, rather hesitantly, was approaching Gently's table.

'Excuse me, but Jeff said you were out here! It's Chief Superintendent Gently, isn't it?'

Gently nodded.

'My name is Conners and I thought I had better have a word.'

'Mr Conners?'

'Yes—but it's about my son, Peter! I found one of your men waiting when I got home—I'm in insurance and I was out on my rounds.' He looked a little embarrassed. 'It's about last Saturday. I met Peter and his girlfriend in the bar. For some reason that he wouldn't tell me, your man insisted that Peter should report to the police station. I mean why? What has he done? Jeff thought that perhaps I should ask you.'

'Your son and his friend were here on Saturday?'

'Yes, they'd been on a hike and dropped in for a drink. I know I left them here to get on with it, but there wasn't any trouble, was there?'

'No trouble,' Gently said.

'Then—why?'

'Your son is required as a possible witness.'

'But . . . if there was no trouble?'

'It relates to another person who was here and whom we think your son may have seen.'

137

Conners paused, staring. 'You mean—?' He made a gesture in the town direction.

'Yes.' Gently nodded. 'And I trust your son will make himself available.'

'But—good God!' Conners looked shattered. 'I had no idea it could be about that.'

'But your son will be available.'

'Yes, of course. I told the man he'd find Peter at his place of work. That's the newsagent's in the High. Good lord, I think I need another drink!'

He took off in the direction of the bar. Gently sat a few moments longer. Did he really want to hear the testimony that Conners's son was going to give them . . .?

* * *

'Well, you know—I can't be certain! We didn't go out there to watch that bloke.'

They had had to wait a full half-hour before Potton ushered Peter Conners into the office. Twice Eyke had gone through to reception, twice had returned to drum his fingers on the desk. But the young man had been out, it appeared, delivering evening papers, and wasn't easily run to earth.

About eighteen, with a pony-tail hair-style and a ring in one of his ears. He stood uneasily before the desk, a little flushed and reluctant.

'You saw him when you went out, did you?'

'Yes. We . . . we had just been talking to Dad.

138

But it was crowded in there, you know, so . . . Well, it was Pat's idea, going out!'

'It was just him out there?'

'Oh yes.'

'Do you remember where he sat?'

'Over by the door.'

'And what about you?'

'Well, Pat—you know!'

'Yes?'

'Across the other side,' Peter Conners said. 'By the gate.'

'By . . . the gate.' Eyke leered at Gently. 'And that's where you stayed till the pub closed?'

'Yes . . . I suppose.'

'You suppose?'

'Yes . . . I mean! We had to leave when the landlord came out to lock the gate.'

Eyke nodded sapiently. 'And when would that have been?'

Peter Conners looked hot. 'Well . . . around eleven.'

Eyke leaned back. 'Now', he said, 'we come to it. This is what we really want to know, Conners. The man who was sitting out there with you—just what time did you see him leave?'

'I—I told you! I couldn't be certain.'

'Oh, come on now, Conners!' Eyke said. 'You were out there snogging with your girl-friend, you just couldn't wait to see the back of him. I'll bet you had an eye on him all the time and after he went you really got heavy.'

'I—he just went! He was there and then he wasn't.'

'He had to pass you, my man. You had to ease off while he went. How soon was it?'

'I . . . well! It could have been . . . perhaps tennish.'

'Tennish.' Eyke fixed him with his eye. 'Would that be a little after, or a little before?'

'I don't know. I didn't look at my watch!'

'And that's it, is it? The best you can do?'

Conners hung his head. 'I want to help you—really! But honestly, I can't tell you any more than that. It was around that time when he left.'

'Perhaps we'd do better asking your girl-friend.'

'Pat? No—she wouldn't know either.'

'So—just tennish.'

Conners stared at the floor and said nothing.

Gently said; 'Someone else you may have noticed. Wasn't another man briefly outside with you?'

'Another man—?' Conners looked up at him. 'Oh—you mean him with the dog!'

'You saw him?'

'Yes. He took his dog to do its thing, across under the hedge. Only he wasn't out there long, not above five minutes.'

'And it was after that when the first man left.'

'Yes, straight after that.'

'Straight—after?'

'Yes. He drank up and went.'

140

Gently paused. He said; 'I may tell you that this could be important. Can you be quite certain that he left within, say, minutes of the dog-owner's departing from the garden?'

'Yes, like I say. Straight after. He finished his drink, got up and went.'

'Well, well,' Eyke said. 'Well, well. You haven't been wasting our time after all! And you're going to swear to that?'

Conners looked uncomfortable. He said: 'I suppose so. If I have to.'

'Oh, you'll have to,' Eyke said. 'Take him out, Potty, and see to the necessary.'

Potton touched Conners's shoulder and a moment later the door closed behind them.

Gleefully Eyke turned to Gently. 'Game, set and match I'd say, sir! This busts his alibi wide open, he could have been on the job with half an hour to spare.'

Gently shrugged. 'We only know he could have been.'

'So why did he lie about it, sir?'

'He may have thought it safe to, to stay out of trouble.'

Eyke shook his head. 'Sorry, sir, but I can't go along with that! He's got too much to answer to, and this was the last break we needed. Before this we were close to a case, but now it's in the bag. You were saying as much earlier, sir—if we broke his alibi, we were going to have him.'

Gently shrugged again.

141

'Time to bring him in, sir.'

Yes, it was time to bring him in: and he was waiting for them with a packed bag! No matter if Lesley Beresford was lying, or another had bruised the dead poet's head: they had a case, a case to be answered. And the time for action had come.

'I'll send Metfield and Campsey to fetch him. You don't reckon he'll give us any trouble?'

'He won't give trouble.'

'He could be a handful.'

'I would prefer that we brought him in ourselves.'

'Us, sir—? Well, if you say so!'

Looking a little perturbed, Eyke followed Gently.

Gently chose to take his own, unmarked, car, and drove with no haste towards the harbour road. Their progress was interrupted; as they turned towards the harbour, a frantic figure waved them to stop. Gently braked and dropped his window: Elizabeth Simpson ran to the car.

'Where's Chris—what have you done with him?'

'What—?'

'He's gone. You've taken him away!'

'Clarke has gone—?'

'You know he has. Please, please tell me where you've taken him!'

Gently said: 'Get in the car.'

'But I want to know—I've a right—!'

'Just get in the car!'

Sobbing, Elizabeth Simpson struggled into the back.

Gently drove on. He slammed the car on to the tarmac frontage of the timber bungalow. They piled out. One thing was obvious: the Lada estate had gone from the garage.

'The sod—he's hopped it!'

Eyke ran to the door of the bungalow and rattled the handle. Then he launched himself against it, more in anger than with hope of success. Elizabeth Simpson collapsed sobbing on the low wall that bounded the frontage.

Gently said: 'Were you in touch with him lately?'

'Yes—I rang him. He was sure you were coming after him! Then I rang him again later.' She sobbed. 'There wasn't any reply.'

'So you came to look for him.'

'I had to! He—he was sounding so desperate. I thought if I could talk to him—' Sobs choked her for a moment. 'But he wasn't here!'

'Have you any knowledge of his intentions?'

'No, he didn't tell me anything.'

'Or where he may have gone?'

'No, that's why I thought—' Her tearful eyes met his.

Gently shook his head.

'Then where—?'

'I'm afraid we need to talk to your friend,'

143

Gently said. 'If you have the smallest idea where he might be, it would be advisable for you to tell us.'

'But I haven't! And if I had—'

'Would you by any chance have a key to the bungalow?'

She had: and after more sobs and hesitations, she handed it to him. Together with Eyke, he made a perfunctory search of the property. It bore signs of having been left in a hurry. Washing-up was left in the sink. A wardrobe hung open, clothes lay on the bed and in the bathroom a towel had been flung on the floor.

'He's hooked it all right, sir. And that's the bloody end for him. That charge will be ready waiting for him just as soon as we feel his shoulder.'

'Take the usual action.'

'Don't you worry! We'll have that bastard before he can blink. He can't be far and if I can use your radio every patrol in the district will be on the watch for him.'

They locked up and went back to the car, where Eyke at once got in touch with control. Miss Simpson still sat on the wall and after a moment's hesitation, Gently returned her the key. Now her tears had been staunched. She took the key gratefully and thrust it away in her bag. She stared up at him, her eyes large.

'And this is it . . . for Chris?'

Gently shook his head. 'Your friend has

acted foolishly. I'm afraid it looks very serious for him now.'

'But he is innocent. I know he is!'

'You—know it?'

'Yes—I mean!' She twisted the bag. 'He would have told me, I know him too well. It's impossible that Chris could have done such a thing.'

'And that's all you mean?'

'Yes. Yes!'

'There isn't a little more you could tell me?'

'Please, no! But you've got to believe me. Chris wasn't there and he didn't do it.'

And she jumped to her feet and ran off, in the direction of the town, leaving Gently staring after her and, finally, shaking his head.

'That's it then, sir,' Eyke said from the car. 'We've got the area covered. If he's heading out of town they could pick him up at the junction.'

Gently said: 'He could have gone to earth here!'

'So we'll just get back and brief the men, sir. But one way or another we're going to have that sod in a cell.'

Yes, it was likely. Clarke was no professional and probably had no plan except that of flight. Gently got back into the car beside Eyke, turned it and headed them towards the station.

There, he rang Sir Tommy, who expressed guarded satisfaction, but swore at the unfortunate Eyke for letting chummie slip through his fingers.

145

CHAPTER EIGHT

He hung on another hour, by which time hopes of an early arrest had faded; no sighting of beige Lada estates, no messages from the men on the ground. On a chance he had rung Beresford, but the painter had sought no sanctuary there; and, on further consideration, Reymerston, who expressed his alarm, but denied all knowledge. Could Clarke, after all, be following some plan that was securing him from surveillance? It began to seem likely. He could not have got far; the alert had been promptly put in place; the small town offered few opportunities for concealment and a single road connected it with the world outside. In time, every last avenue would be explored and the fugitive winkled out, but clearly that time was not to be yet for the moment, Clarke was showing a clean pair of heels.

Gently took his leave of the fretful Eyke. 'Keep me informed.'

'You bet I will, sir! The moment we catch a smell of him.'

Wearily, Gently collected his car and set a course for Heatherings. It had been a long day . . . had it been successful? Without doubt they had made the case against Clarke. Failing other developments, any jury would reward them with a verdict: motive, opportunity they could show in plenty, while the flight of the defendant wrapped it up.

Alongside it there might be queries, but nothing that subverted the facts. Clarke was vulnerable. The case was made. They had but to place him in a dock. Why, then . . .? He no longer knew. He drove, let the road absorb his mind. Perhaps after a good night's sleep what troubled him now would sort itself out . . .

'Andy rang, my dear. He told me . . .'

Gabrielle had a meal waiting for him. He was tired, she could see, and she asked him few questions until after he had eaten and she was pouring the coffee. Then, very briefly, he gave her an account of his day and she listened with a thoughtful gaze till he was done.

'So Sir Tommy is right. And Andy is wrong.'

'At the moment it would appear so.'

'And you are wishing it was not so, yes? You do not like to hurt Andy's feelings?'

'Andy has known Clarke for a long time.'

She nodded solemnly. 'He is most upset. Some mistake, he thinks, there must be, when even you think his friend is guilty. But I say, think of that poor young man, who is dying at the peak of his promise and with such violence. I am sorry for Andy, but not for his friend who is so wicked.'

'West had his failings too.'

'Aha, you say! He is fond of the ladies, yes? That is not a grave fault, my friend, for a young man so handsome and talented. I myself might feel tempted, if only to make you a little jealous. But you would not then wait in the dark and strike him dead, for a few kisses?'

Gently was unable to repress a smile. 'I might just take him aside one day!'

'But you do not kill him?'

Gently shook his head.

'So. How are you feeling sad for this painter?'

'Clarke is also a young man of promise.'

'Ha.' Gabrielle drank some coffee. 'But that is not enough, my friend, it does not excuse what he has done. I shall not feel sad for him and I counsel George Gently not to do so, either.'

'I must think only of the poet.'

'I say yes. We will leave Andy to mourn his bad friend. For you, you are doing your duty and you must not blame yourself for that.'

Gently sighed and finished his coffee.

'And now I say bed,' Gabrielle said. 'Tomorrow, perhaps, is another long day and till then you shall forget these troubles.'

He nodded assent. Of course, she was right. He was allowing himself to become too involved. Feeling happier, he smoked a last pipe, tried to steer his thoughts away from the events of the day.

'Now—we go up?'

Their bedroom overlooked the Walks and always retained the faint scent of heather. He fell asleep almost at once and spent the night in deep, dreamless slumber. That was, until some time after dawn, when a shake of his arm awoke him.

'My dear—it is the telephone!'

He dragged himself out of sleep and into his slippers. The nearest instrument was in the hall and, still drowsy, he hastened down the stairs to take it.

'Yes . . . Gently?'

'It's me, sir. Eyke. I'm sorry to have to wake you up, sir, but you did ask me to keep you informed.'

'You've got Clarke?'

'Well, not exactly, sir! But we have found his car. It was down at the harbour, at the sea end, stuck in out of sight behind a shed.'

'At the harbour . . .'

'That's right, sir. About the last place we looked.'

'And . . . no sign of Clarke?'

'Not yet. But I've got the men on it.'

For a moment Gently was silent.

'Don't know what you think about it, sir,' Eyke said. 'But I'm wondering, you know! Do you reckon we should have the drags out?'

Gently said: 'What's the state of the tide?'

'It's ebbing now, sir. But we wouldn't know when . . .'

'For the moment, just keep observation. And I will be with you as soon as I can.'

'Yes, sir. Sorry, sir. I didn't want to pull you out like this.'

In fact it wasn't so early, either; sun was

already on the dewy lawn. He replaced the phone with an effort and climbed back up the stairs. On the landing Gabrielle was waiting.

'They have found him then—this painter?'

For a moment, he could only shake his head.

After a pause she said: 'Good. So I will go down and make some coffee.'

* * *

It was barely an hour later when he parked by the patrol-cars on the jetty, and by then the sun was riding high and flashing on the wavelets of the outpouring ebb. Men were stationed along the bank, their faces towards the moving water: one at the far end of the jetty. Eyke was waiting for him by the cars.

'Any sign?'

Eyke shook his head. 'I've been on to the harbour-master, sir. He reckons it wouldn't matter when he went in, he would have been carried out to sea by now.'

'Did no one see him park down there?'

'We've spoken to a fisherman who may have seen him. He was just bringing his boat in and thought he saw a bloke up there beside a car.'

'Let's take a look.'

Eyke led him over the waste ground that neighboured the jetty. It ended in marram dunes overlooking the beach where, next to the jetty, stood a derelict hut. The Lada had been parked behind it, invisible except from the

150

dunes or the jetty. The latter was at a higher level, but easily accessible from below. Gently checked the doors of the car. It had been left unlocked, but with no key in the ignition.

'Do you think he came here meaning to do it, sir?'

Gently shrugged: impossible to say. Perhaps something like it had been in the mind of the artist when he drove to that spot, and concealed the car. Or—it may not. His immediate object may have been to escape the attentions of authority, to put himself out of their reach while he considered his next move. And . . . after that? Had the hopelessness of his position driven him at last to an act of despair, to the final solution waiting there in the waters hastening by the jetty?

'Do we know if Clarke owned a boat?'

'No, sir. I thought about that. The harbour-master says he used to have an old dinghy, but he got rid of it some time ago.'

'The fisherman was the last person who might have seen him?'

'He's the only one we've spoken to, sir. He came past here around six p.m., so Clarke was still alive and kicking then.'

'And he didn't know we had broken his alibi.'

'Only a matter of time,' Eyke said. 'He must have guessed we would get there in the end. You said he was all packed and expecting to be arrested.'

Yes: but guilty or not, was Clarke the man to

take this way out? Was there that weakness in his character that made him unable to face what awaited him?

Frowning, Gently stared back up the harbour, past the fishermen's huts, the distant moored yachts. Marshes and the common bounded them, and further still a footbridge gave access to the opposite bank. To Walderness. To ... Could not that thought have entered Clarke's mind? That across there lived a friend whom he could trust, and expect to offer him sanctuary? He had concealed himself and could wait till darkness arrived to further his plans, and then, under cover of night, could have stolen down the bank and across the bridge. It was possible: and Reymerston wouldn't have jibbed; was sold on the belief that his colleague was innocent. While might there not be other such friends, of whom as yet they were not informed ...?

'Do you reckon it's worth calling the drags out, sir?'

Gently shook his head. The harbour-master knew his business.

'Or there's Air-Sea Rescue, sir.'

'I think we can forget all that for the moment. Keep a couple of men down here and for the rest, concentrate on possible witnesses. I have a call to make in Walderness and I'll see you later at the station.'

Eyke stared. 'You think he didn't jump, sir?'

'I think that's the line we should be taking.'

152

'So . . . he's still around?'

Gently nodded. 'And while you're at it, keep an eye on the bungalow!'

He went back to his car and drove. Though just across the river, Walderness was nine miles round by road. It was still early and only after repeated ringing at the door of Reymerston's house did the owner appear, clad in a dressing-gown. He beheld Gently in some amazement.

'Thought you were the milkman, old lad!'

'May I come in?'

'Why not? Ruth's still in the bathroom, but she'll be along presently.' Then the amusement faded from his eyes. 'Is this something serious?' he said.

'I think it may be.'

'I see. But you had better come in, just the same.'

Was there sudden caution in his manner? Gently followed him into the house. Upstairs, he could hear some water flushing, but otherwise there was silence. Reymerston led him through to the lounge and stood a moment with his back to him.

'It's . . . Chris, is it?'

'I think you know the answer.'

'Yes. And I wish I didn't.' He turned. 'I am never going to believe this, George, not even hearing it from you.'

'I'm afraid the case is now very strong.'

'It can be set in concrete for all I care. I have known Chris for too long and nothing you

153

come up with will ever convince me.'

Gently said: 'Clarke has gone missing.'

'So you were kind enough to inform me.'

Gently said: 'We have traced him to the harbour. We found his car concealed near the end of the jetty.'

'The harbour!' Reymerston suddenly stiffened—was it an act he was putting on? 'You can't mean you are thinking—?'

'We have to take facts for what they are worth.'

'But hell and all!'

'The local police are considering dragging the harbour and possibly calling in a helicopter to extend the search out to sea.'

'Oh my God!' His eyes were wide. 'But you're guessing. You can't be certain.'

'A returning fisherman was the last person to see him. When we found his car it was unlocked.'

'But . . . Chris wouldn't do that!'

'He knew he had a case to answer.'

'And you honestly think . . .?'

'These are facts. We can't turn a blind eye to them.'

'Oh hell!' He turned away, shocked dismay in his expression.

Gently said: 'Of course, there is a second possibility. The unlocked car could be a device to suggest a certain conclusion. Clarke could intend us to think this way to provide him with a chance to make his escape. After dark, it

154

would not have been difficult. He had no need to go back into the town. He had only to cross the footbridge to, shall we say, reach friendly territory.'

'To do . . . what?'

Gently said nothing.

For an instant Reymerston stared in seeming incomprehension, then understanding dawned in his eyes and his head tossed back. 'Come off it, George!'

'He would need shelter and assistance.'

'No, honestly, you can't mean this!'

'And a place of concealment. Preferably remote.'

'Like Archie's cottage, you old so-and-so! But you can put that right out of your head. Archie is down here, you can ask Ruth. So don't waste your time hunting Chris out there.'

'Then . . .?' Gently raised his eyes to the ceiling.

'Search the bloody place, if you must!'

'In so many words, has Clarke been here?'

'Do you think I'd admit it if he had?'

Gently said: 'I want the truth from you, Andy. Men are wasting their time down at the harbour. It could lead to an expensive air and sea search for a body. It could also lead to jeopardy to yourself on a count of obstruction, and I wouldn't be able to prevent it. So, was Clarke here last night?'

'Could I ever lie to you, George?'

'Then, in so many words?'

155

Reymerston shook his head. 'I only wish I could say yes. But no, the poor laddie didn't show up here, whatever else has happened to him.' He turned away again. 'I still can't think the other is possible.'

'Perhaps it isn't,' Gently said. 'May I use your phone?'

'Help yourself. I'll go and get dressed. I owe it to Chris to be around over there.'

After some delay Gently raised Eyke and passed instructions to extend enquiries across the river. Less and less did it seem to him likely that Clarke had taken that fatal decision. And if he had not, then Walderness must have been his obvious route of escape: the town direction held too many perils. The odds were they would find him on this side of the bridge.

'The word's got about,' Eyke told him. 'Beresford turned up at the harbour, him and some of his pals. Looking very upset, he was.'

'Anything fresh?'

'Sorry, sir. But I'm still wondering about the drags. The tide is running slack and we could have a bit of luck.'

As he drove slowly back through the village, Gently became aware of Reymerston's Renault, discreetly tailing him.

* * *

But news there was when he regained the harbour: Eyke had located a second fisherman.

156

This one had been night-fishing in the river, by chance only yards below the bridge. He had had his lines out from ten p.m. onwards, packing up at around two a.m., and the only people he had seen cross the bridge were a couple he knew, soon after the pubs closed. Had he perhaps noticed a man hanging about there? No, it was all quiet after that. Nor had he met anyone later on, when he took his way home down the harbour.

'What do you think, sir?'

Gently shrugged. It was still possible that Clarke had eluded the fisherman: had concealed himself and hung on till it was safe for him to proceed. But the odds were slipping. Was it just credible that Clarke had risked the town route after all?

'We'll still make enquiries in the village.'

'If you say so, sir. I can spare two men. But I reckon we might do better to see what we can find in the harbour.'

'It may come to that.'

Eyke looked grave. 'I'm afraid that's how it's going to wind up, sir.'

The Lada remained where Clarke had left it and near it, Gently noticed, stood Beresford. He was alone. He stood close to the jetty's iron struts, peering through them at the slack water. Gently approached him.

Slowly Beresford turned to meet him with a solemn stare. 'Is there . . . news of him?'

Gently shook his head.

157

Beresford returned his stare to the water. 'I'm never going to get over this,' he said. 'I suppose it is true . . . it was Chris back there?'

'We may never be certain of that.'

'But that's the idea. You were going to arrest him?'

'He had questions to answer.'

'It's the same thing.'

Gently made no reply.

'I can't help it,' Beresford said. 'I feel responsible for what has happened. It was me who brought these people together, who set the tone if you like. It tickled my vanity to have them around, to be admired and looked up to. And now, see what has come of it. The two brightest of them are dead.'

Gently said: 'Should you feel responsible?'

Beresford was silent for a while. Then he said: 'I have to say it again. I can't honestly accept that Chris was your man. Was the evidence against him so damning?'

'The evidence was strong.'

'But . . . enough?'

'The likely outcome would have been a charge.'

'And Chris knew that?'

'He knew it.'

Beresford shook his head at the water.

Gently said: 'You will have talked to your son. He may have told you what he wouldn't tell me. Could it be that it wasn't Clarke whom he saw entering the shrubbery that night?'

'Not Chris!' Beresford half turned his head. 'Is there a suggestion it was someone else?'

'I am asking you.'

'Then . . . I can't help you! Lesley told me. only what he told you. He saw a man whom he didn't recognise slip out of the shadows and into the shrubbery.'

'He would add nothing to that?'

'No.'

'And you felt able to accept his word?'

'Good God, he's my son, isn't he? Why would Lesley want to lie to me?'

'Perhaps . . . to protect someone?'

Beresford scowled at the jetty.

'You can see my point,' Gently said. 'An identification of that person is critical. If it was Clarke the case against him is complete, and if it was not we must be told.'

'But if Chris is dead, what does it matter?'

Gently said: 'Clarke may not be dead.'

'Not? But you know he is! Why else would that fellow talk of dragging the harbour?'

Gently said: 'There is a strong possibility that Clarke left his car here as a red herring. He may well be alive and have gone into hiding. We are of course taking action on that assumption.'

Now it was at Gently that Beresford was scowling! 'And all this about Lesley—are you saying he had a hand in it?'

Gently ghosted a shrug. 'I may have formed the impression that not only your son has the desire to shield Clarke.'

'You mean—me too?'

Gently said nothing.

'This is the end,' Beresford said. 'The pluperfect end. Because I'm convinced that Chris isn't guilty, I'm to be accused of helping him to make his escape. You should write fiction too, Chief Superintendent Gently. Quite obviously you have a turn for it.'

Gently stared at him but made no answer.

'Take your men and search my place,' Beresford said. 'You have my permission, search it top to bottom! If you find Chris there you can arrest me too.'

'You have no knowledge of where I might find him?'

'This is too much,' Beresford said. 'I'm off. And if poor Chris gets away with it, there'll be no one happier than me.'

'And ... there is no other whom your son might be protecting?'

'Oh!' Beresford spat. 'Oh!' He stamped away to the parking, got into a car and drove off.

Gently let him go. Just then Reymerston's Renault had appeared from the direction of the town. Reymerston clambered out, stood looking about him, spotted Gently and hastened over.

'Look, old lad!' He wriggled awkwardly. 'I'm not sure I want to tell you this! But I suppose I must. I've got a fellow in my car who thinks he

160

knows where you can find Chris.'

Gently stared. 'Is it Lesley Beresford?'

'No, but you're not far off the mark. It's his cousin Darren, you remember? The pal of young Ambrose who bust his mum's car. It's a bit tricky, because he doesn't talk much yet, but I think I got the right idea. I stopped off in town for petrol and found him by the car when I came out.'

'Did he say where he thought Clarke was?'

'He can still barely string two words together. But he does know something, I'm sure of it, and you can bet he's got a down on poor old Chris. So, I'm doing my duty, I've brought him along to face the maestro. But go easy on him, old man. That crash has left him in a sorry state.'

He led the way back to his car. Sitting in it was a fresh-faced youth with rounded features. As they approached he jerked himself from the car and stood watching them nervously, as though ready to dart away.

Smilingly, Reymerston went up to him and laid a friendly hand on his shoulder. 'It's all right, Darren lad! This copper is an oppo of mine. Gently by name and gently by nature— you can treat him as though he were your dad.'

The young man fixed Gently with staring brown eyes.

'You are Darren Woodrow?' Gently said.

He nodded.

'You have something to tell me?'

He nodded again.

'About Christopher Clarke?'

His mouth was working and he was struggling to get something out. At last it came '. . . beach.'

'You saw Clarke on the beach?'

A decided nod.

'When was this?'

Another struggle. Then: '. . . night.'

'Would that be last night?'

The nod.

'And—would you have seen where he was going?'

The nod.

'Can you tell us where?'

The struggle this time was more prolonged. Finally he pointed with wavering finger towards the town, and then to himself. '. . . show.'

'He went into the town?'

Now the nod was a shake and the pointing more vigorous. '. . . show.'

'Fine,' Reymerston said. 'You're doing fine, Darren lad! And you can show us where Chris went?'

The nod.

'Do you know if he's there now?'

The struggle. Then: '. . . think.'

Reymerston glanced at Gently and sighed. 'I'm afraid it fits, old lad,' he said. 'Chris didn't come my way. He went up the beach. After dark, he could very well have slipped along

162

there.'

Yes: and Gently was cursing himself not to have tumbled to it before. By the beach, Clarke could have bypassed the town and gained open country beyond. And then . . .? He stared at the unfortunate Woodrow.

'We'll take my car in case I need the radio.'

'Just—the three of us?'

'For the moment.'

'Perhaps that's best,' Reymerston said.

* * *

At Gently's car Woodrow hesitated, but at last was persuaded to take his seat. He belted himself in at the second attempt and sat with the staring eyes fixed ahead. Reymerston, who sat behind him, kept his hand on the young man's shoulder. As Gently backed and drove away he was aware of a low moaning sound from beside him.

'Easy, lad!' Reymerston murmured. 'You're in the safest pair of hands in Suffolk.'

But the moaning continued as they ascended into the town, passing the green and the gateway to Beresford's house.

'Which way now?'

Woodrow pointed. He was indicating the road that traversed the Front. Very slowly, Gently drove along it, keeping Woodrow in the corner of his eye. At this hour the beach below them was well-populated: in the hours of

163

darkness it would be deserted. Till late there was life at the café on the pier, but that was an obstacle easily avoided. They arrived at the pier.

'Where now?'

Tremblingly, Woodrow pointed straight ahead. There the Front ended in a car-park behind marram dunes and beach-huts.

'Here . . .?'

He shook his head.

Gently drove to the end of the car-park. Marram dunes hemmed it in, rising beyond to the sandy cliff-tops. And still Woodrow was pointing ahead, to a rough track that penetrated the coarse grasses. Gently heard a gasp from Reymerston.

'Oh lord—no! Chris would never be such a fool!'

'You know where that track leads?'

'I bloody do. It takes you to the bungalows that used to be there.'

'Used to—?'

'I believe there is one left. The rest have gone over the cliff. The last couple who lived there tried to hang on, but in the end the council found them other accommodation.'

'But . . . there is one left.'

Raymerston groaned. 'If Chris is there, he must have taken leave of his senses.'

Gently turned to the staring Woodrow, who merely kept pointing and nodding his head.

'Let's go.'

They climbed out of the car. At once Woodrow darted away down the car-park, stopped once to gaze back at them, then vanished into the road. Reymerston watched grimly.

'The poor young sod. He was on the way to success like his friend. Then first his accident and now all this. You would think there was a curse on Beresford's gang.'

'Just show me this bungalow!'

'If it's still there. It was March when they evacuated the tenants.'

It was still there. But only just. A climb of a few yards brought it into view: a modest timber structure with a balcony: and the latter already jutting out into space. In an overgrown garden roses were blooming and honeysuckle still clung to the walls. A dilapidated gate hung open and bore a name-board: Ocean View.

Reymerston hissed through his teeth. 'Chris can't have come here! The next puff of wind will have it over.'

'Hold back,' Gently said. 'It doesn't need two of us. You stay here by the gate . . .'

'Let's just call him!'

Gently shook his head, advanced cautiously up the weed-choked gravel path. The front door was unlocked. He pushed it open. It gave on a hall that led through to the balcony. He went in—could he hear a creaking? Open doors on either side revealed empty rooms. He advanced a little further towards the balcony,

165

pushed open a door that gave access to a kitchen.

Then: 'That's bloody far enough!'—The voice came from somewhere on the balcony.

'Is that you, Clarke?'

'Just stay where you are, mate! If you come out here we'll both be gonners, they'll be digging our bones out of the beach.'

'Was that your intention in coming here, Clarke?'

'Why not? What else have you sods left for me?'

'You mean to do away with yourself?'

'Just stay where you are, Mr bloody Gently!'

'Chris, you idiot!'—At the sound of their voices, Reymerston had run into the hall. 'Come back in, you damned fool, it isn't safe to be out there!'

'You too, Andy! So come and get me.'

'If I have to, I will!'

And before Gently could stop him, Reymerston rushed through on to the balcony. There were ominous creakings. Gently threw himself backwards. But the doom of the bungalow was not yet. In a moment Reymerston reappeared, dragging the unwilling Clarke after him.

'You ass. You stupid ass!'

'Couldn't you have left me out there, Andy?'

'No I couldn't. This isn't the way. You've just got to face up to things, Chris.'

'You know they've got me where they want

166

me.'

'And now you've made it worse for yourself, you nitwit!'

Gently said: 'Let's get out of here. And Clarke, I take it you don't mean to give trouble.'

Clarke stared at him sullenly. 'And if I did?'

'Then certain steps will need to be taken.'

He didn't give trouble. They marched him out of the bungalow and down the track to the waiting car. At the entrance of the car-park a furtive figure hovered, watching them, but then quickly turned its back and hastened away. Clarke had seen it. He swore to himself and after that kept his mouth tight shut.

CHAPTER NINE

'I suppose now it is inevitable?'

Clarke had been booked in, Eyke advised, and the necessary steps taken to call off the hunt. Reymerston, who had accompanied them into reception, had pressed Clarke's hand emotionally as the prisoner was being led away.

'Keep your chin up, old lad! We'll all be batting for you, you know.'

'Don't waste your time, Andy.'

'It isn't over yet, laddie!'

But Clarke had merely shrugged and pulled his hand away. And Reymerston had hung on in reception until Gently returned from the office.

'Let's go for a drink. We both need one!'

'He . . . he'll be getting a lawyer, will he?'

'Whatever the regulations provide.'

'I mean, if it's a question of money . . .'

Gently pushed him out into the street.

Not far away was the Horseshoes and into it Gently steered the unhappy Reymerston. He glanced round the bar as he entered it and yes, there was the table by the window looking towards the common. He carried their drinks to it. From there, if Lesley Beresford was to be believed, Clarke had sat watching the amorous poet lead Elizabeth Simpson towards those distant, convenient pastures. And what had he said? That West would regret it! Perhaps, at that moment, West's fate had been sealed. When, later, at the soirée West's behaviour became intolerable, the climax was reached and the inevitable followed. Could doubt yet remain? Clarke's flight set the seal on it. Nothing now was left that would trouble any jury . . .

'Do you think he really meant to do it?'

'Throw himself over?'

Reymerston nodded. 'I would never have thought it of Chris, but if he did have this thing on his conscience . . .'

Had he meant it? At the harbour he had left a set-up clearly intended to suggest suicide and following that, had placed himself in a position of some jeopardy. Perhaps he had been toying

168

with the solution, first as a deception, then as a possibility . . . or had he merely observed their approach to the bungalow and hoped a search would stop short of the threatened balcony?

Reymerston drank several pulls of bitter. 'He couldn't know we would trace him out there,' he said. 'I don't think he would have jumped. He was using the place as a hide-out, giving himself time to think what he could do. That's more like the Chris I know. He wanted to be out of your clutches for a while.'

'And then—he would have given himself up?'

'Probably. If he couldn't think of anything better.'

'As . . . for instance . . . applying to a friend?'

'Well, he didn't,' Reymerston said. 'You old so-and-so.'

Gently drank. Reymerston's interpretation had to be the most likely. The unlocked car left by the jetty suggested an element of planning. It was intended to call off the hunt, to provide opportunity for escape. If that had failed, as seemed probable, the odds were that Clarke would have surrendered himself. Yet, he had attempted it: and that before he knew that his alibi had been disproved.

Reymerston sighed into his beer. 'Just his lousy luck that a pal of Ambrose's should have spotted him! If it had been a delinquent like me I would probably have kept my mouth shut. I nearly didn't haul Darren along to you and I

169

doubt if he would have come on his own.'

Gently shrugged.

'So what happens now? Will you be giving poor Chris the third degree?'

'He will of course be questioned.'

'Yes, I can imagine!'

'And his replies noted.'

'I bet.' Reymerston swigged and toyed with his glass. 'How long,' he said. 'How long do you reckon?'

'How long . . .?'

'How long will they put him away?'

Gently shook his head. 'That will be up to the court,' he said.

'But . . .?'

'He has to expect a life sentence.'

'Oh Lord, the poor devil!' Reymerston said. 'But with good behaviour, how long?'

'He may be out in ten years.'

'Ten . . . bloody years.' Reymerston's gaze turned to the window. 'Ten years without paints or canvases and nothing to stare at but prison walls. Perhaps he should have jumped.'

Gently drank. Reymerston threw back the dregs of his glass. They sat a while longer, silently, the custom in the bar building up about them.

At last Reymerston pushed back his chair. 'I had better have a word with Alec,' he said. 'He'll still be thinking Chris did it down in the harbour. At least I can reassure him on that. And for better or worse, he will want to know

170

the part his nephew played in Chris's arrest.'

Gently said: 'Have a word with young Lesley.'

Reymerston stared. 'You think he does know something?'

Gently said: 'Nothing he wants to tell me. But with you he's on a different wavelength.'

Reymerston shook his head. 'You've got a nerve!' he said. 'And if he did spill to me I might not tell you. But I suppose it doesn't matter now, it will just be tidying the loose ends for you.'

'It may help us shorten the process.'

Reymerston shook his head again. And left.

* * *

'Take that chair, Clarke.'

The final scene in Eyke's office was set. Behind the desk Eyke sat himself, with Gently to his right, a shorthand-writer to his left. The painter was ushered in by Potton, who then took up a post by the door. Sullenly, Clarke advanced to the chair placed for him before the desk. He glanced at the shorthand-writer, a comely WPC, but kept his eyes averted from Eyke. And Gently he totally ignored.

Eyke said: 'I think you know the situation, Clarke. Certain testimonies have come to our notice. They conflict with the statement you gave about Saturday and suggest you may have more to tell us. But before you do that, it is my duty to issue you with a warning.' And Eyke duly gave the warning, with the shorthand-writer scribbling it down. 'You understand what I say, Clarke?'

Clarke merely glared at him.

'Right, my lad,' Eyke said. 'So now we'll get down to it. But first, there's a little matter to be cleared up. It has been reported that you made threats against West and that one day he turned up with a bruised face. Have you any comment to make on that?'

'Yes—get stuffed,' Clarke muttered.

'Is that an admission?'

'I said get stuffed!'

Eyke shook his head. 'This sort of attitude isn't going to help you, Clarke,' he said. 'We're talking about the evening of last Thursday week. That evening someone beat him up. And around then you had been heard uttering threats about what you would do if he kept chasing your girl-friend. Can you deny that?'

'Yes, I bloody can!'

'We have the testimony of a witness, Clarke.'

'So the louse is lying.'

'And that's your only answer?'

'Just get stuffed!' Clarke said.

Eyke looked at Gently. Gently said: 'I think you know who that witness was, Clarke. The incident occurred in the bar of the Horseshoes, where you were sitting by the window with a friend. You had just seen West and Miss Simpson pass by on their way to the common

172

and you made a rather unwise remark to your companion.'

'Rotten Lesley—he told you that?'

Gently offered no reply.

'Yes, the bastard! And I thought—' He glowered at the desk in front of Gently.

'Do you still deny it?'

'Why not?'

'It is evidence that may be given in court.'

'Yes, and of course they'll make the most of it—that I couldn't wait to settle with Amorous!'

'So—it was true?'

'Oh damn!' Clarke's stare rose desperately to Gently's. 'Look, one says these things, but it doesn't have to mean—I was only letting off steam in there! Lesley saw them too and I had to say something. It didn't mean I was going to do for the sod.'

'You were just letting off steam.'

'Yes—somebody believe me!'

'And . . . later. On that Thursday evening?'

'I didn't touch him. If someone did, keep looking, because it wasn't me.'

'Not you.'

'No. Write it down! I never touched Amorous and never meant to.'

'Yet someone did.'

'Write it down! Even when I was drunk I wouldn't have done it.'

Gently nodded. Eyke said: 'But you did utter threats—you're admitting that, are you?'

Clarke glared at him. 'Just what I said. And

173

if you don't like it—get stuffed!'

Eyke glanced at the shorthand-writer, who scribbled. 'Right,' he said, 'sonny-boy. Now we're coming to it. On Saturday you took off from Beresford's in a huff and we've got all the testimony we need on that. Young West was still going strong with the girl-friend, he was up in the clouds and she was up there with him. It looked like he'd got it made with Liz Simpson and you were being shoved to one side. Wasn't that the picture, Clarke?'

Clarke looked as though he might jump from the chair. Potton moved towards him: in the end, Clarke merely sat rigid and glowering at Eyke.

'Yes,' Eyke said. 'That was the picture. And you couldn't take it any more. But there was nothing you could do about it right then, so you just picked up your gear and scuttled. Wasn't that how it went?'

'You bastard!'

'Don't write that down,' Eyke said. 'You scuttled, Clarke. West had eased you out and you couldn't bear to watch it any longer.'

'It isn't true. Liz hadn't fallen for him!'

'Oh come on, now,' Eyke said. 'She might have told you that tale later, but there wasn't much doubt at the time, was there?'

'You're twisting it—you're twisting everything.'

'At the time you knew well enough where you stood.'

174

'I knew—! She was trying to tell me, to tell me all that was meaning nothing.'

'But still you cleared out?'

'All right, I'd had enough.'

'Because you knew it was true and that you'd lost her.'

'No!' This time he half rose from the chair and Potton had to lay a restraining hand on his shoulder. He relapsed, groaning. 'Oh hell! It doesn't matter what I say, does it?'

Gently said: 'The previous evening you had discussed the situation with Miss Simpson. I understand you had her promise that she would end her association with West.'

'You've . . . talked to her?'

Gently nodded. 'By her account, the affair was settled. But Saturday evening, of course, was a special occasion with West, his moment of triumph. And Miss Simpson felt obliged to go along with it. She supported him during the signings and, reluctantly, took part in the play. She did her best to make her attitude impersonal, but his own conduct may have obscured that. To even an impartial observer, it may have appeared that she was in love with him.'

Clarke's eyes were wide. 'And you're saying that I—?'

'To you the events might appear even more poignant. She had so lately given you her promise that she intended breaking it off with West. And now she was betraying that promise.

175

West's attentions and his success had overcome it. She was too weak. To West she was available whenever he chose to pay court. And that was the impression you took with you when you departed with such haste from the proceedings.'

'But—it bloody wasn't!'

'You can deny it?'

'Yes, I sodding-well can! It wasn't like that. I knew damn well that Liz was trying to shove him off. She didn't want him—even I could see it. All the time she was giving him the cold shoulder. But then that lousy play started and I couldn't stand that, I'd seen enough.'

'It was the play you were escaping from.'

'Read the bugger, then you'll see.'

'From your disgust at what it involved her in.'

'Yes—and her having to do it in front of me.'

Gently nodded. 'So you departed with no thought of her having betrayed you, merely to escape from a painful situation.'

'Because I wanted to puke—and that's bloody all!'

Gently glanced at Eyke.

'Nice try,' Eyke said. 'And I'll bet you've talked it all over with the girl-friend. But I still like the other way best and I've heard nothing yet to make me change my mind.'

'You—won't believe me?'

Eyke shook his head. 'We hear so much in this game, sonny. And this is only the

176

beginning. You've got a few more things to answer yet.'

'But—!'

'Save it,' Eyke said. 'And stop swearing in front of the lady. We've got you leaving that meeting with West still alive. Now we want to hear how it goes after that.'

'You—!' He was nearly off the chair again. But Potton firmly pressed him back into place.

* * *

Gently said; 'You may smoke if you wish to.'

Clarke glared at him but didn't reply. He was sitting as Gently had seen him before, with clenched fists pressed against his thighs. His build gave the impression of power, of one who could handle himself when it came to trouble . . . but of such a one who would reach for a weapon, when it came to dealing out retribution? Along with the build went strong features, a prominent nose and determined jaw. In the eyes, an alert intelligence. But just now all they exhibited was anger . . . and fear.

Eyke had Clarke's statement in front of him. He glanced through it, then pushed it aside.

'The Brewer's Arms,' he said musingly. 'Not your usual pub, was it, Clarke?'

Clarke said nothing.

'The last pub in town,' Eyke said. 'And about as far from Beresford's place as you could make it. All that way to drink a pint. Could there just have been some other reason?'

Clarke glared, but still said nothing.

'Yes,' Eyke said. 'A likely spot. If something was going to happen back at Beresford's, being seen at the Brewer's might well have its uses.'

'Listen, you bastard,' Clarke snarled. 'I only went in there by chance—not for any frigging alibi! All I wanted was a quiet drink.'

'A quiet drink,' Eyke said. 'But at a pub where the barmaid happened to know you.'

'I didn't know that!'

'Oh, come on,' Eyke said. 'You met her at one of your exhibitions.'

'How would I know where she worked?'

Eyke shook his head. 'I think you would,' he said. 'A handsome female like Miss Collins. There'd have been a little chat when she was looking at your paintings.'

'Oh God—I didn't even remember her!'

'But she remembered you,' Eyke said. 'When you came in, but not when you left. And that is what interests us, isn't it?'

Now the fear was most prominent in Clarke's stare and the fists were biting into his thighs. He snarled: 'I told you when I left—it was around closing—it was getting on for eleven.'

'Easy,' Eyke said. 'Easy. You don't think we took your word for it, do you? A little matter as important as that? We're not quite so stupid, boyo.'

'But it's true!'

'That's what they all say. Which is why we have to hunt up witnesses, and why now and then we light on one.'

'Oh bloody hell!'

'Yes,' Eyke said. 'Is it coming back to you now? That couple of snoggers in the garden, who took a table as far from you as they could get?'

Clarke snatched his face away.

'The table by the gate,' Eyke said. 'The gate you left by, sonny. Just after the man brought his dog out for a wee.'

'But it was later—!'

'Straight after,' Eyke said. 'And those are the very words of the young man's statement. Straight after the man took his dog back in you drank up and left.' Eyke gazed at Clarke with narrowed eyes. 'And you know when that was, sonny-boy? We've talked to that man. He didn't wait till near closing. He was out there at a quarter to ten. And that was when you left the Brewer's Arms, Clarke, and not an hour later like you've been telling us.'

'Look—there's got to have been a mistake!'

'Somebody's made one,' Eyke said.

'That couple! They wouldn't have noticed . . .'

Eyke shook his head.

'Then they're lying!'

'No.' Eyke eased back. 'You may as well face it, Clarke,' he said. 'Your alibi's gone up the spout. You had plenty of time to get back to

179

Beresford's. And I'm going to be generous. If you tell me you didn't mean to knock West off I'm going to believe you. It wasn't till you saw him take the girl-friend into the shrubbery that you had that rush of blood.' His eyes stared into Clarke's. 'Wasn't that how it happened—when you saw him cart her off in there? You saw it and you snapped, Clarke. When she left, you went in and dealt with him.'

There was terror in Clarke's eyes. 'No!'

'Why bother to go on denying it?'

Clarke stared and stared. He gave a wrenching groan, then hung his head and stared at his fists.

Gently said: 'There can be no doubt now, Clarke, that you left the Brewer's Arms before you said. Suppose you accept that and give us your account of what happened after you left.'

'But . . . who's going to believe me?'

'Take your time and tell us.'

'But what's the bloody use?'

Gently shrugged. 'It would not have been improbable if you had returned to meet your friend when she left Mr Beresford's,'

He groaned afresh. 'And you think I did that?'

'Take your time,' Gently said. 'Somewhere you went after leaving the Brewer's. You have a right to give your own account.'

'It won't do me any good!'

'Still . . .?'

Clarke's fists burrowed into his thighs. 'For

180

what it's sodding worth!'

'Yes?'

'I walked down to the beach. I went home that way.'

'By the beach . . .?'

'Yes, the bloody beach! I was never any closer to Alec's place than that. I wanted to be quiet, away from every bugger, and that's what I did. I walked home by the beach.'

Eyke snorted. 'A nice one!' he said. 'And of course, you didn't meet a soul, did you?'

Clarke glared at him.

'Did you?' Gently said.

'You know I sodding didn't! There's no one down there at that hour. Even up on the promenade I saw nobody. I . . . well, I sat a while watching the sea. There were lights out there, could have been a fisherman—but don't worry, he couldn't have seen me! I don't know why I'm bothering to tell you all this.'

'And that's the tale?' Eyke said. 'You were never near Beresford's?'

'That's the frigging tale!' Clarke snarled.

'But you were out of the Brewer's by a quarter to ten?'

'If those sods say so—I didn't look at my watch!'

'Right,' Eyke said. 'Right.' He looked at Gently, who shook his head. 'So we'll just amend your statement, Clarke, to take in these interesting little points.'

'And—bloody then?'

181

'Then it will be time to consider your future, my lad.'

Potton touched Clarke's shoulder. Clarke jumped to his feet. He stood quite still, staring at Gently. 'I didn't,' he said. 'I bloody didn't. Tell Andy. Tell them all! I know you're going to put me away for this, but I didn't. I didn't do it!'

'That's enough,' Eyke said. 'Take him out, Potty.'

'Believe me. Please believe me!'

'Out,' Eyke said.

'Please!'

'This way, sir,' Potton said.

The WPC collected her notes and followed them out of the office. Gently felt for his pipe, Eyke for a cheroot; then, on second thoughts, Eyke rang for coffee.

* * *

'A near thing,' Eyke said. 'Very near. For a time there I thought he was going to come clean. But perhaps he will when he's thought it over, sir, and that was just his last fling. He must realise he doesn't stand a chance.'

Gently blew smoke and drank coffee. 'There is just one angle left to cover,' he said.

'Sir?'

'The probability is high, but still we can't place Clarke at the scene.'

Eyke frowned. 'I can't see that it matters, sir. Not now his alibi has gone kaput. And along

182

with his trying to fake a suicide and do a runner on top.'

'It still rests on probability. And there was at least one possible witness.'

'Young Beresford, sir?'

Gently nodded. 'And Miss Simpson couldn't have been so far away.'

'She will never talk, sir! And I doubt whether he will, with his people all on Clarke's side. But we can have him in again—we shall need his statement about Clarke making threats.'

Gently said: 'He was on the spot. And his behaviour raises a few questions. He was clearly in a nervous state and he went out of his way to detain Johnson. On the face of it, he was expecting trouble out there and wanted to prevent any interference. If West was about to receive a thrashing, that was agreeable to Lesley Beresford.'

'So he's lying when he says he didn't know who he saw, sir.'

'It could go a little further than that.'

Eyke gulped coffee. He said: 'You aren't still thinking—?'

'Let's say it is still on the cards,' Gently said.

Eyke drank some more and regarded his mug. 'I'm seeing it like this, sir,' he said. 'Young Beresford did see Clarke out there and if we can get him to talk, so much the better. But if we can't, no matter, we still have Clarke where we want him. And I have this feeling that sooner or later, Clarke is going to give in and

183

confess.'

Gently shook his head.

'He's no fool, sir. And it could get him a reduced sentence.'

'Don't rely on it!'

'Oh, I shan't, sir. But once or twice he was getting close to it.'

Gently shrugged, puffed, finished his coffee. Minutes passed. Potton reappeared. He brought the amendment to Clarke's statement, so brief that it barely occupied a couple of sentences. Eyke scanned it with satisfaction and passed it to Gently.

'So. Shall we have him back in, sir?'

Gently said: 'It's your case. I'm here only in an advisory capacity.'

Eyke paused, frowning. 'You think I shouldn't, sir?'

'My advice would be to hang on.'

'You mean—until we've talked to young Beresford?'

'His evidence may well be material.'

Eyke thought about it but shook his head. 'We can tackle him afterwards,' he said. 'He won't run away. And then there's Sir Tommy— any time now he's going to be on that phone. Now that we have our hands on Clarke, Sir Tommy won't say thank you if we hold back.'

'It is your decision.' Gently shrugged.

'Fetch him in,' Eyke said to Potton.

The WPC resumed her station with a fresh pad and sharpened pencils: Clarke was ushered

184

back in and reinstalled on the chair. He glared at Eyke: Eyke stared back.

'You have been warned, Clarke,' he said. 'But in case you didn't take it in I'm going to repeat the warning.' He repeated it. 'And now listen carefully to this.' He administered a word-perfect charge, that the said Clarke, at the time and place specified, had, with malice aforethought, attacked and killed one Ambrose West. Then, after a pause, he added; 'Have you anything to reply to the charge, Clarke?'

Clarke spat at him, 'You lousy bugger!'

'That attitude isn't going to help you, Clarke—'

'Get stuffed, you sod. You've bloody got me and that's all that matters to a scab like you.'

'I'm warning you, Clarke—'

'And I'm tired of your stupid warnings! I've nothing to lose and you know it. You'd got me set up from the start.'

'Unless you control yourself—'

'Crap on it. And crap on you too.'

Gently said: 'Do you still plead not guilty?'

Clarke's glare turned to him. 'You bastard! And Andy said I could trust you—if I was innocent, you would see me clear.'

'Is that a yes?'

'Get stuffed!'

'I'll take it for a yes,' Gently said. He glanced at the WPC. 'Write it down. Mr Clarke pleads not guilty to the charge brought against him.'

185

'I'm not pleading anything!'

'Write it down.'

Clarke spat in the direction of the WPC.

Gently said: 'Now, what happens next. You will, of course, be detained in custody and tomorrow you will appear before a magistrate and a solicitor will be appointed for your defence.'

'What bloody defence!'

'The defence of your plea. And in the meantime enquiries will continue. If evidence should arise that will help your case, we are obliged to bring it to the attention of your solicitor.'

'You're—what?'

'You may depend on it,' Gently said.

Clarke stared at him: the glare was fading. He bit back some response, kept his lips firmly pressed together.

'And now, you are permitted one phone call,' Gently said. 'You can make it now or request it later.'

'Who the hell cares tuppence?'

'Perhaps . . . your friend?'

He shook his head; but then glanced towards the phone. Gently pushed it across to him. But the call was a frost. Elizabeth Simpson was not at home. He hung up with a grim expression and stared a moment at the instrument.

'Just bloody-well lock me up!'

'That call needn't count,' Gently said.

'Just lock me up, I say! It's sodding time I

186

began to get used to it.'

Eyke motioned to Potton. Clarke rose and allowed the DC to attend him out. At the door he paused to give Gently a backward look, then shrugged his shoulders and went.

At that very instant the phone rang and lo!— the caller was Sir Tommy himself. Happily, Eyke passed on the news and his expression gave evidence of congratulations received. He looked round to offer the phone to Gently, but the office was empty. Gently had gone.

CHAPTER TEN

'If Lesley is available, he is required at the police station to provide an addition to his statement.'

Gently had taken his lunch at the Pelican, with its windows overlooking the top of the High Street. As he awaited his order he had seen, across the street, the outside displays of the dress shop taken in and, a little later, two girls emerge from the side door; but neither of them had been Elizabeth Simpson. Small doubt she was aware of the events of that morning. Almost certainly, Beresford would have passed on the intelligence. Also, among reporters besieging reception at the police station had been one representing local radio. He had thrust his microphone under Gently's nose, but had failed to cajole a single syllable out of him . . .

'So you got the fellow, sir!'

The arrest was no mystery at the Pelican. He had seen the waiter chatting to the barman, both with their faces turned towards him.

Then the manager had strolled across. 'They tell me you found him in that condemned bungalow . . .'

No, the arrest was all round the town; impossible that Miss Simpson hadn't heard of it. So . . .?

He had stared across at the shop. It was to her that his mind kept returning. Something she had seen, he was convinced of it, and if not Clarke, whom else would she be protecting? One person stood out. It had needed but a glimpse of him advancing from the steps: she might even have bumped into him as she made her escape from the shrubbery. And she couldn't, daren't, give him away, at least while the case against Clarke remained uncertain. All she could do was to declare her absolute conviction that Clarke could not have been the culprit. But . . . now? With Clarke arrested and charged on evidence that left little doubt of the outcome? Was it possible that she could still hold back and allow her innocent lover to be convicted? If hold back she did there must be only one reason: that Clarke was indeed the man she had seen there. His guilt was supported. No doubt could remain. He was guilty and Elizabeth Simpson knew it.

So he was staring across at the shop, where Miss Simpson hadn't appeared for work. In the end, they would have to fetch her back in and seek to pierce the defence of her hysterical tears . . .

He finished his meal. First, there was another angle to be tackled. He directed his steps to the green, to the gates, past the barrier of red-and-white tapes. He rang and a reluctant Beresford came to answer the door.

'Lesley? I'm afraid he isn't in.'

'Would you know where I can find him?'

'No, I'm sorry. You know these youngsters! They come and go as they please.'

'Was he in for lunch?'

Beresford shook his head. 'Actually, I think he may have gone off with Andy. Andy came to tell us what happened, as I expect you know, and I believe he carted Lesley off for a drink.'

'Would you know which pub?'

'Sorry.' Beresford hesitated. 'Dare I ask if this is anything important?'

'A piece of testimony that we require.'

Beresford frowned and caressed his beard. 'Andy was very emotional,' he said. 'Of course, he was glad that Chris hadn't done what we were all afraid of, but he seemed certain that now it was just a matter of course. I suppose there is no hope?'

'Clarke was charged this morning.'

'No possibility of . . . well, some other culprit?'

'None has yet been suggested.'

'No, but I mean!' He let his frown stray towards the shrubbery. 'You have to allow for our acquaintance with the man. We've all known him for quite a few years now and this is so utterly out of character. And it doesn't help that a nephew of mine turned him in, though Darren had always been close with Ambrose.' He glanced back at Gently. 'Was he making much sense?'

Gently shrugged. 'Sufficient.'

Beresford nodded sadly. 'Even my sister has difficulty in communicating with him. He'll just blurt out a couple of words and back them up with gestures. Was he like that with you?'

'Just as you describe.'

'They say he will get better,' Beresford said. 'But I wonder.' He stroked his beard. 'I may be guessing,' he said. 'But I think I know what you want with Lesley. But you are wrong. He truly didn't recognise him, the man he saw going towards the shrubbery.'

Gently said: 'No doubt you discussed it with him.'

'Well, as much as the silly young fool would let me! And Andy has been having another go at him, but it adds up to the same thing. He saw this man and it might have been Chris, but he simply can't swear to it.'

Gently said: 'It was a clear moonlit night.'

'I know, I told him,' Beresford said. 'But I'd say that was a point in Chris's favour, because

190

Lesley ought to have recognised him, but didn't. Of course you don't want to believe him, but I'm sure he wouldn't lie about it to me. And that would leave us with a total stranger going for cover in the shrubbery.'

'Going . . . for cover?'

'What else? He was scared of Lesley spotting him.'

'In fact, your lurking burglar?'

'It adds up to me,' Beresford said. 'Chris is out. It wasn't Chris. And none of our people were about there at the time. A stranger it had to be and one who didn't mean to be found there. So, tragically, he ran straight into Ambrose and had to take steps to silence him. Doesn't it all fit together?'

Gently stared at him. 'There was another witness,' he said.

'Another . . .?'

'You are forgetting Miss Simpson.'

Beresford's eyes were blank. 'But I thought—?'

'She was there. She was in a situation where she could not have missed seeing an intruder. Till now it has suited her to deny it, but that may not continue much longer.'

Beresford's eyes flickered. 'But . . . if she saw Chris?'

'What she saw may have been some other. Somebody whom, for motives we can only guess at, she also felt it necessary to protect.'

'Some . . . other.'

191

Gently nodded. 'Whom she is protecting.'

Beresford dragged his gaze away. He stared at the shrubbery, the tapes. Then back again at Gently. 'She would be lying, of course!'

Gently shrugged.

'Liz . . . she can have only one motive. It's Chris she is protecting and she'd tell any lie to put him in the clear.'

'You think we should reject any other identification she makes.'

'Yes, I do! She would have to be lying.'

'Though . . . her choice might be credible?'

'How can it be credible? Haven't you got all it takes to put Chris away?' He breathed fiercely. 'Look, I'm sorry, but I've had about enough of this. If there is nothing else you want from me, perhaps we can bring this interview to an end.'

'Just that if you see your son, will you ask him to report to us.'

Beresford's only answer was a scowl as he backed off and slammed shut the door.

* * *

Once again Gently lingered on the steps to run his eye over that scene, the rustic arch behind its tapes, the cover of shrubs towards the end of the house. A matter of timing! A few seconds' difference and the assassin might have escaped Miss Simpson's notice: but it was unlikely. To catch West in the shrubbery, he must have

192

made his move the moment she ran out. A moonlit June evening, with prolonged twilight. The sound of other feet on the gravel. She would have glanced aside, seen the figure approaching, perhaps had a second reason for her flight down the drive . . . And the one who stood, like himself, on the steps? Could any grounds remain for a declared lack of recognition? Gently shook his head; that person was lying; and it remained to be told what his object could be. He was lying, she was probably lying; but between them, the truth must be known.

He lit a pipe and moved on, down the drive and on to the green, where once more a figure caught his eye at the outside tables of the pub on the corner; but this time it was Reymerston who sat there, disconsolately brooding over an empty glass. He raised a feeble hand as Gently approached.

'Don't waste your time, you old devil! I may have got young Lesley worried, but that's the lot. I got nothing out of him.'

'Is he still around?'

'No. He took off towards the common. I think he guessed what it was all about and decided to put some space between us. Very nervous, the lad was. Though in his position, so would I be.'

Gently took a seat at the table. 'You had lunch together?'

'A sandwich. It was drink we most needed,

193

neither of us had much stomach for food.'
Reymerston sighed. 'I did my best,' he said.
'Tried to be matey and all that. Told him it
would do him good to talk about it to a
sympathetic pal. No use. He just got nervous,
said he didn't want to think about it.'

'You went over the ground.'

'I kept trying.'

'Nothing more about who it was he saw.'

Reymerston hesitated. 'I hate to admit this,
but he did leave me with a certain impression.
Every time I brought it up he seemed
particularly nervous, kept telling me he never
really saw the man. Once I asked him outright
if it was Chris and for a moment I thought he
was going to throw up. I don't know what you
would have made of it.'

'Your impression was that he knew it was
Clarke.'

Slowly, Reymerston nodded. 'I'm afraid so.
And young Lesley is scared stiff that he will
have to give evidence against him in court.
That's why he is denying it, no other reason. He
couldn't bear to stand up there and accuse him
to his face.'

'No other reason . . .'

'None I can think of.' Reymerston flicked at
the empty glass. 'So that's it, you old devil. It all
stacks up. Somehow, we have to accept that
Chris did it.'

Gently said: 'We had to charge him.'

Reymerston merely jerked his head.

194

Gently said: 'If it is any comfort, I am still keeping an open mind.'

Reymerston's eyes clung to his. Then he shook his head. 'I can't believe you really mean that! Not after the silly ass tried to duck out. Even I have to give him up after that.'

'It could have been the act of an innocent man.'

'Kind of you to say so,' Reymerston said. 'But. If I still had doubts, my session with Lesley put them to sleep.'

'You are quite convinced it was Clarke he saw.'

Sighing, Reymerston nodded. 'Nothing else adds up. He's your trump card. All you have to do is to get him to talk.'

There didn't seem anything else left to say. Gently thought about a drink, but decided against it. He knocked out his pipe, rose and left Reymerston to brood over the dregs in his glass.

* * *

The common was busy on that fine afternoon, with children and dog-walkers in plenty. Gently kept to the road that bounded it till he reached a spot offering an overall prospect. Behind him was the West house, below the sweep to the marshes and the harbour, while not far distant, away to his left, nestled the bungalow-home of Miss Simpson. That way Lesley Beresford had

195

headed, but the possibility of encountering him seemed remote. On the common, into the remote distance, anonymous strollers occupied the scene, while groups of them came and went about the line of cars parked by the water-tower. But, as it happened, nothing could have been simpler. Gently merely had to turn to scan the green before the houses: there, on the very bench where he had sat with Miss Simpson, lay a prostrate figure, its head cradled in its arms. Gently approached it. The figure sat up suddenly. Lesley Beresford stared at him with frightened eyes.

'Andy—told you I was here?'

Gently shrugged and sat down beside him. Lesley Beresford inched along the bench away from him, sat holding it as though prepared to jump up and run. Unhurriedly, Gently took out his pipe and began to fill it, with the youngster's eyes following every move. Gently lit it, then he said: 'If it is convenient, your presence is required at the police station.'

'At the—!'

'It relates to an addition to your statement.'

'An—addition?'

Gently nodded. 'Regarding an incident you reported to me. The incident at the Horseshoes when you were sharing a drink there with Clarke.'

Was he going to run? For an instant it seemed like it: his arms jerked into stiffness. But then they slackened again and he sat with head bowed.

'I—I was making that up! It wasn't true. I only told you that because . . .'

'Because?'

'Well, you know! You as good as said—it doesn't matter!'

'So you told me a lie.'

'Yes, a lie! I'm sorry, I know I shouldn't have.'

'There was no such incident.'

'No. I made it up on the spur of the moment.'

Gently shook his head. He said: 'The problem is that Clarke admits to it. It was put to him during interrogation and he was able to name you as our informant.'

'But it was all a lie!'

'I think not, Beresford.'

'Yes, I'm telling you!'

Gently blew smoke. He said: 'You were under pressure and let it slip. But it is too late now to withdraw it. And what I'm wondering is if the same pressure was responsible for your sighting of a mystery man. Did you see that man, Beresford?'

'Yes—I saw him!'

'And you still deny all recognition?'

'I—!' The arms were stiffening again, the hands tight on the bench.

Gently said: 'I am sure you appreciate the critical importance of that question. A man has been charged with the commission of the crime

197

and you were situated to provide vital testimony. You saw a man. You saw him enter the shrubbery. At least you admit jumping to a certain conclusion. I think you did recognise the man, Beresford, and that man was Christopher Clarke.'

'No—I swear!'

'You could be in trouble.'

He writhed on the bench, but didn't run. 'You can't make me say it and I'm not going to! I'll never know who it was I saw!'

'Just . . . it could have been Clarke.'

'All right!'

'Or . . . another person. Whom you didn't know?'

'I said!'

'A complete stranger?'

'A . . . Oh God, let me alone!'

He was a mess now, Lesley Beresford, hugging himself, twisting himself away from Gently. Luckily there were no passers-by and only children playing ball in the immediate vicinity.

Gently applied himself to his pipe for a few puffs, then said: 'Of course, there is another alternative. It rests on your word that such a man existed. As yet we have no independent testimony that confirms your account.'

'No—please!'

'It will have to be considered.'

'It's mad—I didn't, I couldn't have done it!'

'The opportunity was there.'

198

'You've got to believe me!' He wrenched himself round, stared wildly at Gently. 'I couldn't have got back—there wasn't time— Paul must have seen me leaving the shrubbery! It wasn't possible for me to have done it, you only have to ask Paul.'

'The timing also rests on your word.'

'No—Paul would have to have seen me. He came out'—he hesitated—'he came out just as Liz was running away.'

'Johnson makes no mention of seeing Miss Simpson.'

'No, because I kept him in the porch talking!'

'It could have been he was later than you are representing.'

'Oh God, believe me. Please believe me!'

Gently shrugged. 'So we'll return to this stranger—the one who may have been Christopher Clarke. At the time, it appears you had small doubt and detained Mr Johnson to assist if there was trouble.'

'Yes, I didn't know . . .'

'But trouble you were expecting.'

'Yes, I mean! If it had been Chris . . .'

'But . . . if another?'

'Look, I just didn't know! I thought it was best, that's all there is to it.'

'You had no stronger reason than that.'

'No!'

Gently sighed and shook his head. He said: 'In so many words, I find it difficult to credit

199

what you are asserting. You are familiar with Clarke, you had been lately in his company, you were aware of his particular appearance that evening. To gain the shrubbery he must have approached to within twenty yards of you and there was a moon to assist your observation. It follows that either you saw Clarke, Beresford, or you saw someone you knew not to be him, and if the latter, then your detaining Mr Johnson appears without motive.'

'But I tell you . . . the moon had gone in!'

'It won't do.'

'Yes, I could barely see him! It was just a glimpse . . . I was watching Liz run off. Then, out of the corner of my eye . . .'

'No, Beresford.'

'Just a glimpse, I tell you! And I thought . . . I couldn't take the risk . . .'

'You saw Clarke.'

'No!'

'Then what was this risk you felt so strongly?'

'I . . . I . . .!'

The arms were straight, the feet shuffled for the leap up. But just then, from the direction of the bungalows, a figure came running, calling for them to wait. Elizabeth Simpson: she arrived breathless, hand pressed against her heart. And now Lesley Beresford did spring from the bench, his gaze fixed on her in anger and fear.

'I was in the garden—I saw you. I've got to talk to you. I must!'

200

'No Liz—no!'

'It's too late, Lesley. It was on the news. They are charging Chris!'

'My father . . . he'll fix it somehow!'

Panting, she shook her head. Then, to Gently: 'He didn't do it—Chris was nowhere near the place. You will have to let him go—I know, I know he didn't do it!'

'Liz, shut up!'

'I know he didn't! I'm sorry, I've kept quiet till now. But they've charged him, and unless . . . it's the only way, Lesley.'

'Liz—please!'

Gently said: 'Would you care to be more specific?'

After a couple of gasps, she nodded. 'I ran into him as I left the shrubbery.'

'You ran into whom?'

'Darren. Alec's nephew.'

* * *

'She's lying!'

Elizabeth Simpson had collapsed on the bench. Lesley Beresford stood desperately before them, eyes fixed on her trembling form. The kids and their ball had gone and none of the strollers were in earshot. A couple of gulls, settled on the grass, provided the only audience just then.

'You can't believe her—it's too ridiculous. Darren was Ambrose's best friend! And don't

201

forget I was there—I can tell you it wasn't Darren!'

'I'm sorry, Lesley.'

'You're telling a lie!'

Miss Simpson simply shook her head.

'Yes—and she'll tell you anything to try and get Chris off. Darren—it's too stupid! Next she'll be saying it was me.'

'Lesley, he nearly bumped into me.'

'Two can play at that game, Liz.'

She looked at him sadly, then shook her head again.

To the gulls, Lesley Beresford said: 'It wasn't Darren. I can tell you who it was.'

'Oh Lesley!'

'Oh yes. If I have to tell him, I will.'

'You don't mean that.'

Lesley Beresford turned a tremulous gaze towards Gently. He said: 'You were right. All along. The man I saw out there was Chris.'

'Lesley, how can you!'

'Because it's true—and I only lied about it for your sake!'

'It's now that you are telling lies.'

'Oh no, I'm not. And he knows it.'

Gently said: 'Before we go any further. Darren Woodrow would appear a most unlikely prospect. I hear from everyone that he was West's friend and could have little motive to wish him ill.'

'Of course he hadn't,' Lesley Beresford said. 'It's utter rot. Who's going to believe it?'

202

Elizabeth Simpson turned her attention to the gulls.

'Well?'

'Perhaps you remember! I told you Ambrose said he had an enemy. I didn't tell you who he said it was, or what had been the occasion of it.'

'She's making this up!' Lesley Beresford exclaimed. 'Always they were the best of friends.'

'Not always, Lesley. Something happened. It happened almost a fortnight ago.'

'Nothing did happen!'

She nodded. 'It was the car accident that happened. An accident that turned poor Darren into what you see now.' She turned to Gently. 'Before that, Darren was one of Alec's up-and-coming protégés. He had published several short stories and was in the middle of writing his first thriller-novel. Alec was sure it would be a winner. Darren read us a chapter at the last soirée. And then, suddenly, everything was over and Darren had become a sort of zombie.'

'But that had nothing to do with Ambrose!' Lesley Beresford broke in.

'I'm afraid it had everything to do with him,' Elizabeth Simpson said. 'It was Darren who took his mother's car, but it was Ambrose who crashed it.'

* * *

'You don't know that—it's just what he told

203

you!'

Lesley Beresford's stance was almost threatening. He had moved a step closer to Elizabeth Simpson and stood crouching, with clenched fists.

Elizabeth Simpson was unmoved. 'He told me and everything bore him out. Twice, I saw Darren following us when we were out for a walk, and once when we went for a drink I caught him peering at Ambrose through the window.'

'But he's like that now. He isn't normal!'

'The expression on his face made me shudder. He blamed Ambrose. He had lost everything and clearly he thought Ambrose was responsible for it.'

'You're making it up!'

'No.'

'It's all a tale to get Chris off!'

Elizabeth Simpson stared at him, then shook her head and turned away.

Gently said: 'West made that admission to you—that it was he who crashed the car?'

'Yes. At first I didn't believe him, because there had been no mention of anyone else involved. But he told me he didn't dare hang on afterwards because he didn't have a licence, and once he had seen Darren getting to his feet he made himself scarce. Two other cars had stopped, so he knew there were people to look after Darren. He managed to slip away behind the hedge and make his way back to town.'

'He had received no injury?'

'A bang on the head, but nothing serious. He went into the first pub he came to and got himself sozzled. It wasn't until two days afterwards that he learned the sort of state Darren was in. He felt terribly guilty, of course, but there didn't seem much point in him making a confession.'

'A . . . bang on the head.'

'Yes. I noticed the bruise and asked him about it. That's when he told me. As I said, at first I thought he was telling me a tale.'

'And this happened when?'

'A fortnight ago . . . about Yes, the Thursday of the week before last. I remember now. We met on the Sunday.'

Gently turned to the wretched Lesley. 'And you knew nothing of this?' he said.

'It's lies—lies!' He almost spat it out. 'Ambrose got that bruise hitting his head on a door.'

'He told you that?'

'Yes and I believed him. And I don't care what she says. It doesn't matter! Darren wasn't there. It was Chris I saw going into the shrubbery.'

'You are prepared to swear to that identification?'

'Prepared! I . . . yes!'

'On oath, Beresford?'

'I . . .! Yes, if I have to!'

'Lesley, you mustn't!' Elizabeth Simpson

205

exclaimed.

'I will, if you go on telling lies about Darren!'

'But they aren't lies, Lesley. Chris didn't do it and you mustn't go on pretending he did.'

Lesley Beresford flung a trembling hand towards Gently. 'Ask him,' he said. 'Ask him! They've got Chris and they've charged him, it doesn't matter what anyone says now.'

'No, Lesley!'

'He won't get off!'

'Lesley, please!'

'I saw what I saw!'

'Lesley!'

'I'm going to tell them!'

Elizabeth Simpson burst into tears.

Gently said: 'Perhaps I should warn you, Beresford, that to lie on oath is a serious offence. If you are in any way uncertain, you had best leave your statement unamended.'

'But . . . if I saw!'

'Did you see?'

For a moment longer, Lesley Beresford stood wildly staring. Then he ducked his head and ran off in the direction of the town.

Elizabeth Simpson sobbed: 'He saw Darren—he knows he saw Darren! You don't believe him, do you—it won't make any difference?'

Gently shrugged. 'Probably not!'

She scrubbed at her tears. 'Please tell me! I held out as long as I could, but when I heard . . .' The tears flowed fast.

Gently said: 'When you are ready, we will go along and take a fresh statement.'

'And then . . . Chris can go?'

Gently shook his head. 'Perhaps not quite yet.'

'Not yet?'

'Clarke is under charge. Your fresh testimony will be given every consideration.'

She stared and sobbed afresh. Then she blurted: 'But I can see him, can I?'

Gently handed her his handkerchief. 'I think it can be arranged,' he said.

CHAPTER ELEVEN

It was arranged; though perhaps very little to the satisfaction of Elizabeth Simpson. In the presence of Gently, Eyke and a WPC, Clarke was fetched into Eyke's office. Clarke was looking grim. He gazed at her, seemingly unable to offer a greeting, and failed to respond with much enthusiasm when she threw herself into his arms.

'Chris, it's going to be all right! They know now—they know!'

'Please Liz!'

'I've told them everything—how I nearly bumped into poor Darren!'

Clarke pushed her away from him. 'You've told them what?'

'It was Darren, Chris. Darren!'

'Darren?'

'It was Ambrose who crashed the car when he got his injury.'

'And you're trying to tell them—?'

'It's true—I saw things! He had it in for Ambrose ever since then. Ambrose knew, he told me. He knew that Darren meant to do something.'

Clarke's stare was incredulous. 'They'll never believe that! Ambrose and him were best buddies. You should have picked on young Lesley, everyone knows he bore a grudge.'

'But Darren was there, Chris. I saw him!'

Clarke glanced furtively towards their audience. He shook his head. 'It's too late, old girl, they're never going to believe that now. You should have come up with it earlier.'

'I couldn't, Chris!'

'It's too late now.'

'Even though it's the truth?'

'Even then. You've left it too late, Liz. They don't want to know.'

'But—Chris!'

'I'm in court tomorrow.'

Weeping, she flung herself back into his arms and this time he didn't push her away. Between sobs she stammered: 'I'm never going to give up, Chris—never, never. Because I know!'

When the office was clear again, Eyke stole a cautious look at Gently. He said: 'She tells a good tale, sir. Such a pity Clarke didn't know

208

she was going to swing it.'

Gently said: 'It shook Lesley Beresford.'

Eyke nodded. 'We'll have him back in, sir. And that's what she's done with her little yarn. Now we'll have what you said we needed—testimony to pinpoint Clarke at the scene.'

'It will be his word against hers.'

'No problem, sir. His fits the facts and hers doesn't.'

'Her account would explain that bruise.'

'So she's been clever. But that's about all.'

Gently said: 'She could prove a stubborn witness, if Clarke's defence produces her at the trial. I doubt if the same can be said of Lesley Beresford. A good counsel might quickly take him apart.'

Eyke hesitated. 'You surely aren't thinking—?'

'I saw his reactions,' Gently said.

Eyke looked away. 'But it is only her word, sir. And even Clarke wasn't taking her in.'

Gently said: 'We can't overlook it. Either way, we must follow it up. On the surface she could be lying to get Clarke off, but while there is a doubt we shall have to pursue it.'

'I can't see how, sir.'

Gently said: 'That car crash happened less than a fortnight ago. Perhaps we can have a word with the officer who attended the accident.'

After a pause, Eyke lifted the phone: 'Locate Jackson and tell him we want to see him in here!'

Jackson came. A young constable, he replied to their questions eagerly. Yes, he'd been patrolling in the area and had arrived at the scene within minutes. Several cars were already pulled up there and one driver, a Mr Green, had recognised the crashed vehicle and the injured driver. The latter appeared to have suffered concussion but otherwise no apparent serious injuries. A Mr Evans, the first to arrive at the scene, had found him wandering in the road by the crash.

'You took statements?'

'Of course, sir!'

'Any mention of some other occupant of the car?'

Jackson looked warm. 'Well now you're asking, sir! Mr Evans thought he saw another person in the vicinity when he first got there. But whether that person was from the car didn't occur to him and we didn't bother to include it in his statement.'

'Did he describe him?'

'Not really, sir. We put him down as a bystander who didn't want to get involved.'

Eyke dismissed him with a flea in his ear. Reluctantly, he turned to Gently.

'They could have been right, sir. It may have been just a bystander happy to leave it to someone else.'

Gently shook his head. 'It fits too well.'

'You mean . . .?'

'We shall have to bring in Woodrow.'

Eyke said nothing.

'Do we have his address?'

Eyke nodded. 'It's in one of those terraces on the Front.'

* * *

But collecting Darren Woodrow wasn't to prove easy. Gently took his own car and found a niche near the house. A woman of around fifty answered his ring and stood firmly planted in the doorway. A handsome woman, fashionably dressed in a flowered two-piece with lace trim: she eyed him angrily, up and down, and spared a ferocious glance for Eyke.

'So what do you two want?'

'Is your son at home, Mrs Woodrow?'

'Suppose he is?'

'Regretfully, his presence is required at the police station.'

'Ha!' Her stance became yet firmer. She did her best to stare him down. 'Don't think I don't know who I'm talking to,' she said. 'My brother spoke to me on the phone. He warned me of your stupid, your laughable ideas about Darren, and to expect a visit like this. Well, my son is not available, now or on any other occasion.'

'I'm afraid we must insist, Mrs Woodrow.'

'You can do that till you're blue in the face.'

'We may need to make an official arrest.'

'Arrest Darren! I can't believe what I'm

211

hearing.' She drew herself tall. 'Listen, you fool. You can put Darren right out of your head. I can speak for Darren. At the time of my brother's soirée on Saturday he was here, right here, in this house. He was watching television the entire evening—he is still capable of doing that. At no time was he out of the house, so you can just go back to your jealous painter.'

'We must still talk to your son, Mrs Woodrow.'

'I repeat, he is not available.'

'You would be well-advised to co-operate.'

'Thank you. Your advice is noted.'

And, without another word, she closed the door and they heard the sound of a bolt being shot.

Eyke grimaced at Gently. 'What do we do now, sir?'

Gently shrugged. 'It may come to a warrant.'

Eyke looked grave. 'But you heard what she said, sir. If she sticks to that we can forget about Woodrow.'

'I think the lady is well able to tell a lie.'

Eyke shook his head and stared at the shut door.

However, as they stood irresolute, a silver Mercedes slid into view, hesitated briefly, then mis-parked with its wheels on the pavement. From it jumped Alec Beresford. His scowl as he faced them was grim.

'Is Darren in there?'

'We believe so.'

212

He wasted no time in further enquiry. Hastening to the door, he rang on the bell what appeared to be a code, a long and three shorts. At once the bolt was withdrawn and the door thrown open.

'Alec—thank God!'

He pushed her back in and the door closed again. Briefly, they could hear the sound of voices, then the sound retreated into the house. Eyke stared at Gently.

'We'll wait,' Gently said. He backed off and went to lean against his car. After pausing, Eyke joined him. In silence they waited, regarding the house. Time passed: and Eyke grew restive.

'You don't reckon, sir—?'

'Beresford is no fool.'

'I mean—while we're stuck out here! These houses have their garages at the back.'

Gently shook his head. 'Just wait.'

And finally their waiting was rewarded. The door opened again to reveal Beresford, his sister—and Darren Woodrow. His uncle had him by the arm; the young man was staring with vacant eyes. His mother was dabbing hers with a lace handkerchief; and Beresford's scowl was grimmer than ever. He led Darren to Gently.

'Here—for what it's worth! I suppose his mother is permitted to come with him?'

'If she wishes.'

Darren was thrust into the car, his weeping mother beside him.

213

For a moment Beresford stood scowling at them, then strode across to the Mercedes. He pulled out behind them as they drove away.

No words were spoken on the drive to the police station.

*   *   *

'There's going to be trouble, sir. I can feel it in my bones!'

At the station, it had needed all Beresford's influence to persuade his sister to remain seated in reception. It was her right to be present when her son was being questioned—she would appeal to a magistrate—to Sir Thomas! He wasn't well and they were inhuman to be questioning him at all! Her assertion that her son had been at home at the critical time was clearly on the tip of her tongue and only furious scowls from Beresford had persuaded her not to repeat it. In the end, she had relapsed into dramatic hysterics and was left in the charge of her brother and a WPC.

'You'll go easy on him, will you?'

Just how much did Beresford know? Unquestionably, it was to his father that Lesley Beresford had run from the common. Beresford was advised of Elizabeth Simpson's admission and had reported it to his sister; but wouldn't he have demanded that his son made a clean breast of his knowledge, to himself? Those scowls at his sister had been revealing:

214

she had been warned not to proceed with her version.

'I'd sooner you handled it, sir!'

The set-up in the office was the same as for Clarke. Potton guarded the door, the WPC was in her place, it remained only for the principals to take their seats behind the desk. On the hot-seat before it, Woodrow sat sprawling, his empty eyes seeing nothing. Was it even remotely possible to obtain a sensible response from him?

Gently took the seat of honour, spent a moment studying that huddled form. 'Darren? Darren Woodrow?'

There was a flicker in the staring eyes.

'I think you remember me, Woodrow. This morning your friend Andy introduced us.'

Another flicker ... was it fear? Now, his hands were in motion. Gently waited. At last, with the usual struggle, it came out: '... helped.'

Gently nodded. 'You assisted us, Woodrow. We were wanting to talk to Christopher Clarke and you were able to take us to him. And now we would like your help again. It is about a night I am sure you remember. The night when you borrowed your mother's car. You do remember that night, Woodrow?'

The eyes jerked to his. Jerked away. '... don't!'

'But I'm sure you must do, Woodrow.'

'... don't!'

215

Gently nodded. 'I think you remember that night very well. Another friend of yours was with you. It might even be he who suggested borrowing the car. Your best friend. Ambrose West. At his request, you let him drive it.'

'. . . didn't. No!'

'He drove the car, Woodrow.'

'. . . didn't!'

'I think he did. Unfortunately, he was inexperienced. He hadn't passed a test. The result was that he had an accident and you received a bad knock. Because West had no licence he ran away and left the responsibility with you, and you were in no state to deny it. People blamed you, when they should have blamed him.'

'. . . wasn't. No!'

'They blamed you. You were the cause of your own misfortune. Of the injury that left you unable to work, to mix with others, to write your book. You were blamed, but he was to blame. And the success he was achieving made it the more unbearable.'

'. . . didn't . . . wasn't!'

'I think so, Woodrow. From being your friend, West became your enemy.'

'. . . no!'

Gently nodded. 'And in the end, West had to pay for the wrong he had done you.'

Woodrow dragged at his knees. '. . . Chris. Chris!'

'No, Woodrow. Clarke we have talked to.'

216

'. . . yes. Chris!'

Gently shook his head.

'. . . isn't. . . wasn't. Chris!'

He flung himself round in the chair, hugged his knees, moaning. The WPC looked uncomfortable: Eyke was staring steadily at the figure on the chair.

Gently said: 'On Saturday night the soirée was being held at your uncle's. You couldn't attend it, Woodrow, you weren't able any longer to play your part there. Yet, you couldn't keep away either. I expect you knew what was due to take place—that your enemy, once your friend, would be riding high in the triumph of his success. The place drew you to it. You loitered in the grounds, perhaps spied on the proceedings through a window. And all that you feared was in progress and your enemy being feted to the skies. Clarke was another one who couldn't take it. You saw him stalk out in disgust. But you continued there, Woodrow, waiting for the meeting to break up.'

Gently paused. Woodrow was staring up at him with rounded eyes. Saliva dribbled from his twitching lips, but all that emerged was a low moan. Gently said: 'You watched people leaving. You had positioned yourself at the corner of the house. It may not have been evident to you, but your cousin was in the porch, seeing people off.

One of the earliest to leave was Miss Simpson, whom you were aware that West was

217

seeking to seduce. He followed quickly after her and, after a few words, succeeded in leading her into the shrubbery. Three girls left next, but you may not have noticed them. For you, his success with Miss Simpson was the ultimate provocation. You pursued them into the shrubbery, nearly colliding with Miss Simpson as she ran out. And in the shrubbery you took your revenge, Woodrow. You plucked out a stake and struck West to the ground.

Whether you intended killing him remains an open question, but yours was the hand that struck him down.'

He paused again. 'Have you anything to say?'

Woodrow was struggling, his mouth working. 'Well?'

'. . . Chris . . . Chris!'

Gently gazed at him, shook his head.

'. . . Les . . . Les!'

'Your cousin Lesley?'

His head was bobbing. '. . . saw!'

'He saw Clarke?'

The head went on bobbing. '. . . Chris . . . Les saw!'

'He saw him enter the shrubbery?'

'. . . saw!'

Gently said: 'He saw someone, Woodrow.'

'. . . Chris . . . saw!'

'I don't think so, Woodrow.'

'. . . mn, mn . . . saw!'

'And that is all you have to tell us?'

'. . . mn . . . Les saw!'

He ducked his head and went on moaning. The WPC rested her pencil.

Eyke stirred. He said; 'Perhaps we could have a word outside, sir?'

They went out to the passage and Gently led them to the end most remote from reception. From there, they could hear the low tones of Beresford, interspersed by the sobs of his sister.

Eyke whispered: 'This is getting us nowhere, sir! You can see what he's like. Unless we can get young Beresford to talk, we've got no grounds for letting Clarke off the hook.'

Gently said: 'I doubt if Miss Simpson is lying.'

'But the way she's placed, it isn't good enough, sir. And if Woodrow's mother stands by what she told us, then we're left holding thin air. You made a good case in there, sir, but unless he breaks down we're back where we started.'

'Perhaps—not quite.'

'It looks like it to me, sir.'

'There may be a card still to play.'

'Sir—?'

Gently nodded in the direction of reception, then led the reluctant Eyke towards it. Their entry produced a sudden silence. The eyes of brother and sister fixed on them. The lady was still seated, lace handkerchief in hand, with Beresford, beard tilted, standing beside her.

It was he who spoke. 'Well?'

'Your nephew has answered a certain question,' Gently said.

'You mean—?'

Gently shook his head. 'As you may imagine, questioning him is attended with a degree of difficulty. But of one thing he seems to be quite positive, that we have made no mistake in charging Christopher Clarke.'

'He . . . told you that?' Beresford's eyes were large.

'He seemed advised that your son could testify to Clarke's presence.'

'Bloody Lesley!'

Gently shrugged. 'We shall, of course, need to question him again.'

Beresford's eyes switched to his sister, who immediately burst into tears. For a moment he stared at her, then fiercely back again to Gently.

'Can I talk to him—to Darren?'

Gently nodded. 'I think you may.'

'Then, for Christ's sake lead me to him!'

His sister's tears flowed. But she said nothing.

* * *

'It's me, Darren. Your uncle.'

Discreetly, Gently and Eyke took their places again.

At a nod from Gently, the WPC turned to a fresh page in her notebook. Beresford had

220

planted himself before his nephew, had roughly jerked up the latter's face to confront him. Woodrow gazed with bewildered eyes, then eyes that widened with fear.

'Darren, this can't go on!'

'... Uncle ...!'

'And don't play games with me!'

'... mn. .. no!'

'It's too late for that now. And let me tell you your mother agrees with me.'

'... mn ... mn ...!'

'So you listen, my boy. You've got to stand up and be counted. There's no other way out of this now and I'll be ashamed if you go on trying. You understand? It's time to speak up and be the man I always thought you.'

'... mn ... mn ...!'

Beresford knelt beside him. In a softer tone he said: 'You've got nothing against poor Chris, have you? Chris, who did that good sketch of you which your mother had framed and hung in the parlour? He's a decent fellow, Darren. And they've got him locked up here in a cell. We can't let it go on. You mustn't keep on telling them it was he who did that to Ambrose.'

'... mn!'

'It's not good enough, Darren.'

'... mn. Chris!'

'I've talked to Lesley, you know.'

'... Chris!'

'In a minute, I shall really be angry!'

Woodrow jerked away from him, hung his

221

head.

Beresford aimed a glance at Gently, then tipped his nephew's face back towards him. 'Listen,' he said.

'Listen, Darren. We know you weren't at home Saturday night. You went out straight after tea and weren't in again till midnight. Your mother was waiting up for you, but you could offer no explanation. She says you were in more of a state of nerves than ever and she thought you might have been in a fight. So, where were you?'

'. . . mn. . . out!'

'Yes, but out where, Darren?'

'. . . mn . . . a walk!'

'It won't do, my lad.'

'. . . mn, mn . . . the beach!'

Beresford shook his head. 'Tell me!'

Woodrow wrestled clear of him: hid his face. Beresford pulled back, scowling. 'I'm ashamed of you, Darren,' he said. 'Ashamed. I thought you had guts. Now it seems you haven't.'

'. . . I . . . I . . .'

'No guts,' Beresford said. 'You can't stand up and face the music. All you can do is lie and let an innocent person take the blame for you. And you a nephew of mine! The son of my sister and a father who was worth ten of you. What do you think he would say if he were here and could see you now?'

'. . . no . . . Uncle . . .!'

'Uncle indeed! You have lost your claim to

222

call me that.'

'... Uncle ...!'

'No. From this moment on, you are no longer a nephew of mine.'

'... but ...!'

Beresford's head shook determinedly. 'You are a liar and a coward, Darren. On Saturday two people saw you up at the house when Ambrose died. Lesley saw you. Liz saw you. You were making into the shrubbery as she came out. God knows what you had against him, or why you set about him like that, but you did, and Ambrose is dead and all you can do is try to blame it on Chris. And I am still to own you as my nephew and the son of my sister's husband?'

'... please ... please ...!'

'A coward. A liar.'

'... please ...!'

'And your mother in tears out there?'

'... please!'

Tears were also streaming down Woodrow's face. He gazed at his uncle, his lips working, a feverish flush on his cheeks. Then suddenly he threw himself into Beresford's arms and clung to him, sobbing helplessly. Beresford clasped him tightly in his bear-like embrace.

'No more—no more lies?'

Woodrow's head shook violently.

'It was you who did that to Ambrose?'

The shake changed to vigorous nodding.

'And you're going to tell them?'

He sobbed, but still nodded. Beresford turned to look at Gently.

Gently said: 'Perhaps it's time his mother saw him. You can use this office.'

'It may be best. And—then?'

Sadly, Gently shook his head.

* * *

Surprisingly, there turned out to be few problems in getting a statement of confession from Darren Woodrow. Either the impediment to his speech had been faked or the recent crisis of emotion had done away with it. After the interview with his mother and uncle he appeared still distressed, but a good deal calmer, and was able to answer questions rationally, though with some nervous hesitation. He had nothing to say about the motive for his actions and responded only with silence when asked about it. But, for the rest, he gave a satisfactory account and seemed almost anxious to have nothing left out. Whatever his mental state had been at the time, there seemed little question about its adequacy now. Meanwhile, elsewhere, Lesley Beresford had been fetched and, under his father's eye, had given his amended statement; while Metfield and Campsey had been despatched to requisition the contents of Woodrow's wardrobe. It remained then only to summon Christopher Clarke and to inform him that the charge against him was being dropped. He heard the intelligence in staring disbelief but, when it sank in, turned on Gently.

'But—Darren! You can never charge him?'

'Appropriate action will need to be taken.'

'But he isn't normal. I've seen him! They'll never let you get away with it.'

'I said, appropriate action.'

'Oh hell! I think I'd sooner—' He shook his head. 'I suppose you must know what you're doing. But if it had been anyone else but you!'

However, relief at his release soon took precedence and he was anxious to press his apologies—if he had spoken out of turn to Gently, it must lie at the door of the situation he had been in.

'All the time Andy told me to trust you, but I couldn't see it. I felt so sure you were against me.'

Beresford had driven his sister home, and then had returned to the station to seek Gently.

'I suppose—there's no hope?'

Gently shook his head. 'I'm afraid we must detain your nephew in custody.'

'In a cell—here?'

'The same cell that Christopher Clarke has just vacated.'

Beresford scowled at nothing. 'At least, I suppose we have to be grateful for that!' He stroked his beard. 'And young Lesley?'

Gently hunched. 'I think we can let it rest with his statement. For a while, my colleague

225

had other ideas, but I pointed out the pressure your son must have felt under.'

'And . . . me?'

Gently's shrug was repeated.

'It's a stupid business,' Beresford said. 'There's no sense in it. It shouldn't have happened. The real culprit is Gwendolen, for not locking up her car-keys. Isn't that how you see it?'

'No blame . . .?'

'Well, a tragedy that shouldn't have been!' He tugged at his beard. 'And now . . . Is there a chance of my having a word with him?'

Eyke looked tired and fed up. 'I've just been on the phone to Sir Tommy,' he said. 'He isn't too pleased, sir. He thought we'd got it sewn up and now we drop Clarke and nick a relative of his missus. I had to tell him. A full confession, and now we've found stains on chummie's clothes. I don't think you're his favourite person, sir. He seemed to think it was time they retired you.'

'Sir Tommy never minces his words.'

'If I were you I'd stay clear of him, sir.'

'Have the Wests been informed?'

'Not yet, sir.'

'I think they deserve to be kept abreast.'

Outside, it was another clear evening, with the moon just beginning to gather power. Gently, too, felt a weariness upon him. He got in his car, began to drive.

Was there blame somewhere? Perhaps

Beresford had put his finger on it—Gwendolen should have locked up her keys! Otherwise . . .?

He suddenly felt thirsty and stopped at the Brewer's for a quick half.

CHAPTER TWELVE

Darren Woodrow was subsequently charged, though on a reduced indictment of unlawful killing, and strings were pulled that enabled the trial to be dealt with early in the autumn sessions. In his summing-up the judge was brief and laid emphasis on the prisoner's evident remorse, and expressed his satisfaction at being able to dismiss Woodrow with a five-year suspended sentence. The media were eluded: Woodrow was smuggled out of court and driven to a secret address, from whence he was carried off by his uncle to join the rest of the family in a rented villa in the south of France. The event was handled deftly from first to last, with perhaps some small assistance from a moody Sir Tommy.

But the Wests, as could be expected, were less inclined to let the matter be buried so conveniently. Their son's funeral offered a platform to which the media was freely invited. In addition, the display window of West's office was utilised for an exhibition: photographs of Ambrose, along with his book and his manuscripts, presided over by the Buddha from his study. Flowers were left there, the local press featured it and the exhibition continued through the autumn. The book, meanwhile, sold out and went first to a second, and then a third, printing.

'I don't know!'

Andy Reymerston had the book in his hand one sunny autumn day. They were in the garden at Heatherings again, the Reymerstons, the Capels, Gently and Gabrielle. The Doctor had brought his violin with him, but so far had left it in its case. A faint breeze was bringing them perfume from the Walks: butterflies clustered on buddleia and the Michaelmas daisies.

Gabrielle said: 'You do not like?'

Reymerston shook his head. 'Perhaps I'm no judge! he said. 'But modern—so-called—poetry always reminds me of a quote from Byron. It relates to Wordsworth "Who, both by precept and example shows, That prose is verse, and verse is merely prose".'

'Poor Ambrose!' Tanya Capel laughed. 'So he wasn't a poet after all.'

'I'm merely a painter,' Reymerston said. 'But for me, poetry ended with Keats. It may have lingered with the Victorians and a little later, but then a couple of Yanks killed it stone dead. Pound and Eliot were the assassins.'

'Oh, what nonsense!' Ruth Reymerston exclaimed. 'And Ambrose was a poet, a real one. I adore his poems about Zen.'

228

'He merely stinks of it, as they say. He hadn't learned to Walk On.'

'Well, he convinces me. But you're against all religions, Andy.'

Reymerston sighed and stretched himself on the sun-bed where he was lounging. 'Zen isn't a religion,' he said. 'And in my view, the time has come to purge the human race of myth exploitation. What do you say, George? Isn't myth—squeezing the source of all evil?'

'Oh, don't drag George in!' Ruth Reymerston said. 'It's Ambrose we're talking about, anyway. For me, he is a true poet and I'm sure I'm not the only one here who thinks so.'

'For me, he is—difficult,' Gabrielle said.

'I'm inclined to agree!' Tanya Capel laughed. 'And it's no use asking Henry, because he hasn't read him. That leaves George.'

'George?' Reymerston said.

Gently stirred and tilted his sun-hat. 'Do wake Henry up,' he said. 'It's time he gave us a little music.'

'A right Zen answer!' Reymerston chuckled. 'Tanya, give your husband a dig. And if he has the smallest feel for his surroundings, he will kick off with some Percy Grainger.'

Dr Capel obliged. And he was still Country Gardening when Mrs Jarvis emerged from the house with the tea-tray.

* * *

The Beresfords remained in Cannes through all that winter and the Wolmering soirées seemed to have come to the end of their reign. Reymerston, it was true, sought to revive them by renting a private room at the Pelican, but the spirit was missing, attendances fell and in the end he gave up the effort. Then, near Easter, the Beresfords returned and word went round that all was not lost. Invitations arrived: a date was announced: there was to be a notable reunion of the clan. Doubts were expressed, yet people came, nervously approaching the fatal spot—only to find that, during the interim, the spot had been entirely done away with! Beresford had engaged a landscape gardener and now the shrubbery was no more. Its place had been taken by an open lawn, a fountain and a pattern of flower-beds in the French taste. So different, in fact, was it that its previous form quite escaped the memory, and with it the ghost they had trembled to find there, the shade of that tragic moment. All went well, the soirée succeeded and Wolmering's Bohemia was reinstated.

Darren Woodrow and his mother did not return: a new residence had been found for them, some miles down the coast.

And, in the succeeding June, Christopher Clarke married Elizabeth Simpson.

Brundall, 1996

230

We hope you have enjoyed this Large Print book. Other Chivers Press or Thorndike Press Large Print books are available at your library or directly from the publishers.
For more information about current and forthcoming titles, please call or write, without obligation, to:

Chivers Press Limited
Windsor Bridge Road
Bath BA2 3AX
England
Tel. (01225) 335336

OR

Thorndike Press
P.O. Box 159
Thorndike, Maine 04986
USA
Tel. (800) 223-2336

All our Large Print titles are designed for easy reading, and all our books are made to last.